The First

Book 1 of the Purple Hearted Series

Frances Fleur

HB Publishing House

Blurbs

Whoever said falling in love was easy, lied.

Turning 18, Cora never envisaged her world would fall apart. After an abrupt return to her childhood town, she is thrust back into a life she had so desperately tried to escape. An unexpected meeting, with a handsome stranger, leads to the first kiss of her dreams. The attraction is undeniable. As their lives unexpectedly intertwine, it makes her question everything. Cora tries to navigate this romantic twist of fate. Falling in love for the first time, wasn't anything like she had ever imagined.

The first love is always the most memorable and this forbidden teacher – student love story will leave you wanting more...

Contents

One

The return — Cora

My eyes spring open to an unusual thud. The bedroom is in darkness, and it is suffocating. I don't move, hidden under my quilt, statue still, pretending to be asleep. Is it a dream? Is it a burglar? Clearly, this is how a horror movie starts, the viewer shouting at the television, urging the main character to run and hide in the cupboard or under the bed. I am staying completely still – with the child-like mentality that if I can't see you, then you can't see me. Silence. It is eerily silent.

Am I dead? Have I been stabbed already?

This is what I expect death to be, this quiet. I hold my breath and the hum from the air conditioning floats into my ear, and then a shuffling sound comes closer.

Definitely not dead. I let out a controlled sigh.

Cora, this is stupid.

The shuffling is now in my room. Crap, maybe it is a break-in? I try to slow my breathing, in 1,2,3,4 out 1,2,3,4. I am willing myself not to have a panic attack – stop being stupid but being murdered on my birthday would utterly suck – bloody hell!

"Cora, we need to leave, now!" I sit up in a panic, throwing my quilt on the floor. Nope, not a robber or a serial killer but Dad, and his voice sounds desperate. My eyes wander over to the shadow standing in the doorway.

"Dad? What's going on?" I whisper, just in case it is a dream. I don't want to wake the apartment up again with one of my night terrors. At almost 18, I should be over these experiences, it is getting embarrassing, but they show up when I least expect them. My eyes adjust to the dark, his frame is hunched, and he keeps looking back to the door.

Is he scared? Maybe he heard a burglar?

He strides from the doorway to the switch of my bedside light and turns it on. I quickly cover my eyes, hoping to brace myself from too much light, and let out a yawn. Mission not accomplished, as my eyes squeeze shut from the searing light. I peek my eyes open and look at Dad again. It looks like he hasn't slept, his eyes are bloodshot, and he has either been drinking, crying, or both.

"They know," he mutters. A knot quickly forms in my stomach. He starts frantically opening the drawers on my bedside cabinet, and I can see he has already started packing my suitcase, hence the thud. "Only take what you need. We leave in ten."

Horrified, I jump up and race around the room, fighting an overwhelming dread. If they find him, he will be arrested. This is bad. Bile starts rising in my throat – please do not vomit. If there is one thing I cannot stand in this world, it is vomit. I shoo Dad out of the room and dress quickly, opting for joggers and a vest top with flip-flops, packing as much stuff as I can. My heart is racing for another reason now, a night terror or a burglar seems much more welcome, and I lean my body over the bed, hands clutching the headboard, trying to calm my breathing.

I pause momentarily and inhale a deep breath, willing my heartbeat to slow down, feeling a little shaky.

Calm down, just calm down, Cora.

Deep breath, in through the nose and out from the mouth. Six times according to *Rob Dial Jr's Podcast*. That man can talk and breathe his way out of any situation, and so can I.

Just breathe.

After a minute, I swing back into action. I finish cramming as many clothes into my suitcase as possible, fight with the zip, and I'm ready. I grab my phone from the nightstand and pull the suitcase quickly along the tiled apartment floor, stopping by the front door where Dad is waiting. He is holding onto his phone for dear life, his eyebrows furrowed into a worried gaze. We had spoken about how this could get out, but the job over in the UAE was too luxurious not to take. Paid schooling, double the salary he was previously on, healthcare, a beachside apartment, and a new start, we all needed the new start. We also talked about how he would be discreet, and we talked about how he would be secretive. So, who told the authorities, and more importantly, why?

"How did they find out?" I ask, but Dad shrugs as he stares off into the distance.

"Does it matter?... Ready?" I nod and take one last look around the apartment, mentally saying goodbye. "Daisy?"

"Yeah, yeah, I'm here." My sister emerges from her room, she is only a few years younger than me, but at 16, she is completely different. I am tall, she is small, she has blonde hair whilst I have brown, she has blue eyes, and I have green. I always tease her that she was adopted because we are so different, mind, body, and soul.

"Where are we going?" I ask as I step out into the heat of a Middle Eastern winter.

"We are going back home."

Home. Such a strange word when I don't even know where that is any-more. The flight is uneventful. I watched a documentary on some boy band that rose to success a few years back, but one of the band members killed himself last year some sort of drug overdose. It is pretty depressing, so obviously an interesting watch, pretty fitting for me and my tastes. I even nap for at least 20 minutes.

Many hours later, the plane touches down on the tarmac at Heathrow. I feel my stomach lurch into its actual place, rather than dancing in the sky. I welcome solid ground with relief. It is not that I am a nervous flyer, I just don't like the thought of being 30,000 feet above the ground in a metal tube full of fuel, with several turbo engines close to my body – not to mention the proximity of all the strangers on this flight. I don't know them, they don't know me, they may murder me in my sleep or take over the plane. Irrational thinking, I know, but it is slightly daunting with little sleep and hormonal teenage rage. Plus, I *need* to stop watching disaster documentaries, such as *Titanic* or *9/11*.

Disasters are so awful to watch, but I cannot turn my eyes away. I want to know all the horrible details and why! I scowl over at Dad (who is still snoring away) in the seat next to me. How can he sleep through the whole flight? He didn't even wake up for the meal. Maybe it is an adult thing, no shits given when a person reaches a certain age. What is that age, 30, 40, 50? He looks so calm and relaxed when he was in despair only a few hours before. I smile as his moustache slightly quivers under his heavy, steady breath. We are safe, and that is all that matters. Daisy punches me in the arm.

"Weirdo."

"Ow, Daisy, what the hell?"

"You were daydreaming, smiling, at Dad... weirdo." She goes back to listening to music on her phone.

Cow.

I can honestly say I hate her; she never has anything nice to say. It seems she goes out of her way to piss me off. I sigh and look out the window. The plane is steering its way slowly into the terminal, and I notice that despite the little flecks of water appearing gently against the small, tunnelled window, it is actually beating down hard with rain, lashing and bouncing back up on the tarmac. It barely rained in Dubai. I already miss the consistent sunshine, the warm breeze against my olive skin, the beaches, oh, they were so sandy, the cool water on my feet.

Now, returning to England in January will be a shock to the system. I shiver, anticipating the cold and wet already, and not even the good kinda wet either! I check my watch, 4:30 am, so it is GMT-official: I am now 18. Yay.

Happy birthday to me.

It is not particularly how I thought I would spend my 18th birthday. I had planned a party, *the* party, my birthday party, a poolside one, with an actual DJ, and Alix, the guy everyone crushed on, had said he was coming. After all those months of flirting with each other, this would be my night. My life is officially over; I will never know if he did like me. He had the most piercing blue eyes and a cute Canadian accent that everyone sighed over. He was funny, not the smartest, but his face more than made up for it. I had heard he was an amazing kisser and I wanted to get my lips around his.

Well, there goes a heartbreaking love story never written, damn life! With the rush to leave and return home, I did not have much of a choice – I was forbidden even to text my friend to say we were going, and Dad took my old sim card and snapped it. I feel a small lurch in my stomach about what I left behind, but I try to push those feelings down. It is what I do best, push them down as far as they will go and rage it out later. I keep reminding myself that I am safe now. We all are.

That is all that matters, right?

It has only been just over a year and a half since we left, but all of us driving back to our old house feels oddly comforting. Dad squeezes my leg as he pulls into the drive.

"All right, over there?" I nod, but what can I say?

Soz Dad, today has been a load of massive crap balls, send me back right now, the sun makes me happy. Or, *I didn't realise I had a choice in coming back.* Or, *thanks for kidnapping my arse.*

No… Dad didn't need my guilt right now. It could be worse, Dad could be in jail, and we could be homeless, living on the streets. The police would have taken all of our passports. We would have been stuck and lost. How long are you imprisoned for being openly gay in a country where it is against the law? Before I get out of the car, Dad turns off the engine and looks at Daisy passed out in the back seat, snoring. I swear I can see dribble, the tramp.

He then looks at me, "Cora…" he sighs. "I know this has all been a bit sudden to leave everything… there was always a risk… but this new start here will be good for us." Ahh, Dad, ever the optimist. As I stare into his tired blue eyes, he looks sad, defeated… old. This is definitely what he said last time, before we left to go to the UAE.

"New start?" I moan. "We are back where we started, Dad." He contemplates my words.

"True, but, we tried, and I emailed a few work colleagues. And, well, they have sorted me with another acting headteacher position… this new job, back at your old school. It will be good for us. You said you wanted to come back anyway and apply to the universities in London." I see the worry in his eyes, and I grab my bag and start to open the car door.

"Dad, you don't need to worry, it's all good."

I have to be careful; I didn't want to upset him even more than he already is about the situation. I can see Dad's heart breaking from leaving his boyfriend behind. Cole was and is a great guy, and my dad did find happiness, which is rare, but that seems to have been ripped from him again, as we left him behind. He smiles, satisfied with the answer. I wish it felt that easy, or maybe I am just an excellent actress. I grab my suitcase from the car boot and head to the house.

"Convenient that the renters moved out just before Christmas," he laughs as he nudges Daisy awake.

"Convenient or fate? Who knows." As I enter the house, I try to force some of Dad's optimism in me and re-familiarise myself with the layout. The house is cold and smells a bit musty and broken. I inwardly smile. I think we are all a bit broken today.

Well done, house.

I look over to the sofa where Mum used to sit, passed out drunk or screaming at us about how we ruined her life and how worthless we all were, only pleading for forgiveness the next day, when she'd semi-sobered up. But that was one of the reasons why we left. She almost feels like a thread pulling us back, not letting us have a fresh start for long or a fresh start from her. I cannot wait to crawl into bed. I look at Dad as he walks into the house with his suitcase, Daisy trailing behind.

"Go to bed, birthday girl. We can celebrate tomorrow evening." I smile at him, relieved. I go upstairs and walk into my old room; I don't know what I was expecting, but it doesn't look the same as it did. Smaller, definitely, but it also doesn't feel like mine. My shades of lilac were gone from the wall, replaced with boring magnolia. Even though my oak desk, wardrobe, and drawers are still there, they don't feel like mine either. I look at the bare bed and faceplant, falling asleep almost instantly. I would happily sleep on the floor right now I am so tired. As I close my eyes, I make a mental note to buy new sheets tomorrow, when I am awake enough to care.

Two

The meeting — Cora

♥

Waiting for a friend sucks! I glance at my watch and realise she's now 30 minutes late. What sucks, even more, is that 'so-called friend' said she'd be here soon!

SOON!

I check my phone, but still no text. Maybe it's payback for buggering off to another country for a while, or maybe shite said friend is still rubbish at timekeeping like she has been for the last several years of knowing each other.

I guess things have not changed that much. I knew I should have come an hour later, but I thought 15 minutes would be enough.

Clearly not.

My mind drifts back to Dubai, and how it would now be the middle of my perfect party, and a longing ache crawls up my skin.

Dad disconnected all our old phones immediately in case the authorities tried to contact any of us. He wanted us to go under the radar, and I get it. He is trying to protect us. But if I am really honest, I am pissed. I did not save any of my friends' numbers or memorise any of them either. I barely remember to set my alarm, and nobody emails anymore, it is all text. So that's another thing to add to my shite pile. I wonder what they will think when I don't turn up.

But we are safe, I just must remember that and keep saying it. Thank goodness Dad got me a new sim card today. The thought of not having a working phone makes me feel like I am lost and naked.

My toes start to tingle with what I swear is frostbite and I think I may have hypothermia, but I am not waiting out in the cold in the town square any longer. My hair hates any kind of weather change and it' is starting to widen like a lion's mane, to the point where I will have to go back home and straighten the damn thing again! So, I am making an adult decision, I am going to the pub for a drink.

With the alluring thought of warmth, I walk down the road with a determination to combat my newly-acquired frostbite. I loiter for a moment at the entrance and stare down at my ID.

This is it.

I flip it over and over and over in my palm as if it is gold, knowing that things will change now, at last, I'm 18 years old. Freedom, real freedom. Not the fake freedom, with the fake ID, which sometimes works, and sometimes doesn't. I smile to myself, slipping it into the back of my fitted jeans pocket.

I look up at the sign, 'Nobody Inn', what a great name for a pub. The bitter winter wind whips around me, and I pull my coat tighter. Not quite the warm weather of the UAE, but having a birthday drink legally – the day does have its perks.

I hover on the stone step for a few seconds longer, thinking this is the threshold of 18, this is where life begins (apparently), and I enter the pub a little bit more enthusiastically than a regular, but who cares! Did I already say? I am 18 years old, baby!

The town pub is warm and cosy and is pretty deserted for a Saturday afternoon, apart from a couple by the window and a random guy at the other side of the bar. I slide onto the bar stool casually – like I do this *allllllll* the time. Although I have lived in this town for several years on and off, I have never attempted to go into this pub, or any really, so this is an all-new experience for me. Anticipation bubbles in my stomach at the thought of the future and all the experiences to come and I welcome it with open arms! I reluctantly remove my coat (half expecting icicles to break off) and lay it on top of the stool beside me. A shiver runs through me, crappy winter weather.

Jet lag may kick my arse and I spent most of my birthday on a flippin' plane, or in the car, or sleeping. But I, Cora Wilkinson, WILL celebrate my 18th, even if it is by myself.

I recheck my phone. Stupid so-called friends, clearly pissed at me for leaving, have now got themselves lives and boyfriends, whatever! I don't need friends to have a good time, even though the pang of loneliness creeps into my brain.

NO!

I am a strong, independent woman, yes, a strong independent woman, and friendship is over-rated! The slim bartender returns to the bar and eyes me cautiously.

"Can I have a red wine, please?" A very grown-up drink for a very grown-up me. Do I even like red wine? I think I had some over Christmas, and all the sophisticated actors drink wine in films. Well, I will soon find out. Alcopops are for teenagers!

"Do you have ID?" I try to look slightly offended, but I am smiling inside.

Yes, I bloody do!

I show her my driver's licence, and her eyes scan it, giving me an approving nod and pours the drink. She sets it down on the dark wooden bar, and I pay by contactless. I silently 'cheers' myself by raising the glass into the air.

Happy birthday to me, I am one sexy bitch!

I sip slowly and smile, closing my eyes and savouring the moment, breathing in the old carpet smell, and a hint of oak, yeah, that's how you do it! Adult style. I'm not sure if red wine is for me, but at this moment, I would take anything with alcohol in to warm me up.

"Celebrating?"

A man's deep, smooth voice calls from the other end of the bar, sending a delicious shiver down my spine. He moves his head into the light and gives me a warm smile showing his cute dimples. I eye him over slowly and I catch my breath a little. He clearly has that 'just walked off a photoshoot' look and it's disgustingly beautiful. I lick my lips as they suddenly feel dry and I almost forget how to breathe.

As he clears his throat, I realise the silence has been a little longer than I realised. He is so freakishly hot; I have to stop the urge from fanning myself or doing an over-the-top swoon, which I believe would be totally appropriate right now. I quickly side-check to see if he is not talking to someone else (you know, that embarrassing moment when someone waves at you, or starts talking to you, only to realise it is someone else behind you. That has happened to me far too often than I would like to admit). Nope, it was me, definitely me.

Shite... I have never done this before.

Sure, I love all those romance novels and films, where boy meets girl, boy loves girl and girl loves boy, insert a bit of drama, it becomes resolved and they live happily ever after. But I don't have a script, I don't ever get chatted up and I bite my lip unsure how to answer.

"Yes, I guess I am," as I return his smile, trying to look confident, but then yawn unexpectedly.

Great first impression, Cora.

"I did not realise I was that boring," he jokes.

I recognise his slight Irish twang and I think my lady bits just explode. There is nothing sexier than the Irish accent for me.

"Oh, no, that wasn't... sorry... I am a bit jet-lagged."

He tilts his head slightly in curiosity and some of his light brown hair falls over his face. He runs his hand through it, the sexy hairstyle that has just grown out from a mid-cut. What would it feel like to run my hands through that perfect hair? My mouth pools with water, as if I may be sick. But it's definitely drool, not sick, and not a reaction I have had before. But I welcome it, as I seem to be doing a lot of firsts today. What I wouldn't do to lick him a little.

"Oh? Been anywhere nice?" he asks.

"Visiting the UAE," I reply a little too quickly.

I mean, this is not a lie or the complete truth. I couldn't exactly tell him the exact truth. Even in my head it sounds crazy, my family absconding, and I just want to make myself look good in front of this beautiful stranger, or to make myself feel a bit better about what really had happened. How we dumped and ran from a pretty good life – I was happy with it, for once. Being away from Mum, not worrying about people talking about me at school and the school bitches hurling abuse about my family and me. We had had enough.

But in Dubai, we were just a normal ex-pat family coming out to enjoy what another country had to offer. Now, being pulled from paradise back to rainy, cold England, would people remember me? Would the shame talk start up again? I hadn't even considered that yet, going back to school and facing it all. I bite my lip again, as worry starts to rise. The stranger continues to talk, pulling me out of my darkened thoughts.

"I visited the Middle East a few years back on a stopover to Japan." He grabs his drink, walks around the bar and sits a few seats away from me. "Zach."

"Cora." He extends his hand, waiting for me to shake it, which seems a little old-fashioned and formal. My hands feel a little sweaty, but I shake his anyway, hoping he won't notice. His hand is warm and soft, radiating a small tingle up my arm, making me smile.

"Well, Cora, what are we celebrating?"

Is he coming on to me? Or am I overthinking this?

I stare into his deep, bear brown eyes, and he meets me with an intense gaze. It is magnetic, and I don't want to look away. Or is it a game to see who looks away first – the last one wins a prize of his tongue down my throat?

Well, fuck me!

I feel myself blush, and let out a little nervous laugh, pulling my hand away, some interesting stirrings radiating down in my lady parts.

Well, this is new! I hope it is not wee. Why would I wee myself? Stop overthinking this, Cora.

I squirm a little in my seat, feeling out of my depth.

"I guess...I am celebrating returning home." He nods in approval, lifts his glass, and we clink them together. He smiles again, and we both take a sip from our drinks. I look over my glass at him, trying not to slurp, hyperventilate, or pass out – any excuse just to look at him a minute longer. Taking a slow, deep breath and trying not to over analyse this encounter.

However, do I believe in love at first sight? Because today, I really do. I have definitely seen some beautiful men in my time, but mainly on TV or in magazines. Never in real life... well, actually, that is not true, if I wanted to ogle at beautiful men, I would sit near Gucci or Lois Vuitton and people-watch at Dubai Mall after school.

Now those men, WOW!

I used to pretend to be on my phone or looking for someone, but some of those men had my vagina exploding. Now I have one of those men, right in front of my eyes, talking to me, and I don't know what to frickin' do with myself.

"So, Cora, what do you do? Do you study at uni here?" I raise my eyebrows, surprised. So, he clearly does not think I attend school; he hasn't run away, and wants to talk to me. Another internal smile washes over me. Thank goodness for early puberty, more than average breasts, and many hours of experimenting with the natural look of hairstyles and make-up.

Social media, you rock!

I am so glad I made an effort today. He does not think I am at school. I suddenly find a renewed confidence.

Okay, deep breaths, I got this, let's see where it goes. Remember, strong, independent woman!

"Yes, I do," he looks at me expectantly as if to elaborate, "I want to do something with a music degree, maybe, teaching or performing, I am not sure yet."

Again, not a lie but not the complete truth. I mean, I have looked into some universities, and I know I do want to play music in some form. I kinda need to pass A-levels first, apply to university and also get in. I look him over subtly, and he is older for sure, but how old is he?

"I am a teacher," he responds enthusiastically as his eyes light up. Mid-twenties? Definitely not 30, unless he is having a mid-life crisis and wants to see how young a girl he can pull.

Ewwwww, I sound disgusting. I put that aside: *thoughts – leave me alone to drool over this gorgeous man-god.*

Those eyes, that accent, I am surprised I can put a sentence together right now. I silently high-fived myself for not messing this up. 18 years old really does suit me.

"Really?" Well, that came out a bit too high-pitched, sounding a little bit too keen. I sip my drink to try and calm down, my hand shaking a little, but he does not seem to notice.

"Just coming into my second term, I graduated last year, it has to be said, though, that teaching is... stressful, but I'm enjoying it, and I am surviving." Maybe I overestimated; maybe he is 22 or 23, then? That's only 5 years-ish difference, I can work with that. He gives me a mischievous smirk, and oh, what a beautiful smirk. I stare at his perfect teeth and realise I am giving him a cheesy grin back.

Hide behind your drink, Cora, and calm down a little bit. Older men like composed ladies, not gawking teenagers.

This conversation with a man is a whole new concept to me, like the moon landing, nobody was sure what to expect then, but everyone was bloody excited about it all. Yes, I may be nervous, but this is exhilarating. I take a large gulp of my wine, thinking it will calm my nerves, but unexpectedly choke on it.

"Are you okay?" I cough and splutter the drink over his tight-fitted, grey shirt. I put my hand over my mouth and gasp in horror.

I played that real smooth and cool, not! I can imagine telling our future kids. *How did you meet Dad?* (They would ask.) *Oh, children* (I would respond), *I just coughed all my wine and lady juices over him, it was love at first sight.*

Except that's not what will happen, and I see this may go downhill quickly. I scan the room looking for a swift exit or a hole to jump into from embarrassment, I am not picky, I just need to leave.

I lean over automatically, grab a napkin from the bar and start to wipe it down with my hand and I feel his rock-hard abs. Then it quickly dawns on me that I am touching him up greedily with my hands, and my eyes bulge slightly.

This is not the correct way to clean up the mess I have just made. But my goodness, touching him is such a thrill. His eyes darken and I see his mouth twitch. I snatch my hand away hastily, embarrassed, my fingers tingling from that instant touch.

"I am *so* sorry." I push out the words to try and make them as sincere as possible. He takes another napkin from the bar and wipes down the rest of his shirt. He smiles at me again, seemingly unfazed. "Let me buy you a drink?... It is the least I can do."

"A beautiful girl is asking to buy *me* a drink. How can I refuse?"

He gives me that knicker-melting smirk. I relax a little and the panic subsides.

Does he think I am beautiful?

Small butterflies form in my stomach, maybe I don't need a swift exit or hole after all, maybe all I need is a bed to lie down together on instead. Thinking back to the last person who called me beautiful... it was probably Dad and that was not romantic, obvs. I order a beer and another wine for myself.

A comfortable silence gathers around us, I side glance assessing the drink explosion damage, but it does not seem that bad. I mean who gets to meet a cute guy and spit drink over them? Sounds like a start of a porno.

"So, what do you like to do in your spare time, when you are not study-ing?" Zach asks, breaking the silence.

I think about it for a moment and play the honesty card. "I play the piano and sing, a little." Thanks to Dad's overprotectiveness from birth, he has always encouraged or pushed Daisy and me to take extracurricular activities, music, languages, athletics, all of them (to keep us out of trouble). To be honest, I welcomed it all. A fresh start always gives a renewed sense of identity, and I was interested in learning all about the new me.

However, in the last few years, Dad has stepped up his 'Parent Game', calling his authority, so any small bother and I was grounded. I tried any-thing to drown out the boredom and to meet new friends, but eventually, I settled on the piano society and choir. Singing at after-school clubs was the only relief and the main social activity I had, and if I thought about it, I was pretty damn good too!

"Anything I might have heard of?" He asks.

"It's mainly for myself. I guess I am not quite there yet, you know, with the public performances, the confidence. Maybe someday." I carefully sip my drink and continue thoughtfully. "I just love the whole process of songwriting, the words created, they're so specific. I believe the beauty of it just comes from the soul and can bring someone's passion or feelings alive, and spending hours working out that perfect chord or melody, when finished, gives such an accomplished feeling. And, when someone listens to it, knowing it can result in bringing a person to tears or it makes someone want to dance, or smile, it tells a story… it is beautiful." I respond wistfully and his eyes seem to dance at my confession. Clearly, he likes what I have to say.

"That sounds amazing. I would like to hear that one day," he responds with a mischievous twinkle in his eye.

"You would? Why?"

I realise I am furrowing my eyebrows in confusion. *("Don't frown, Cora, or the lines will be there for life." Yeah, great advice Mum.)* I rub the crease on my forehead instinctively.

"Funnily enough, I teach music, and this isn't a way to come onto you or anything. I really do teach music. I love music, especially live music…

maybe you can let me listen or come and watch you play sometime?" I give a shy nod, noticing he has not even taken his eyes off me. I feel myself blushing again and break his intense gaze.

"So... what about you?"

He smiles and breathes in a little, leaning back on his seat more comfortably to answer the question, clearly showing his trim waist and arm muscles. My gaze wanders over him, and I wonder what he would look like with his shirt off, running my hands down his muscular chest. Would it be hairy or smooth? What would he feel like on top of me? I feel flushed again and lick my lips, clamping my legs shut tighter, feeling a deep throb. He catches me doing this and smirks. He can see I am trying to have eye sex with him.

Shite, am I that obvious? Calm down.

"Erm, well... I like to run. I have completed a few marathons in my time. I write a wee bit, trying to get published with a few children's stories I've written."

"Wow, impressive."

Smart, gorgeous and funny, is this even real? Is this actually happening?

"Are you?" He asks curiously.

"Am I what?"

"Impressed?" I hold his gaze and I feel my heartbeat quicken. He's confident and cocky. I like that too; it's such a turn-on.

"Well, that is a very bold question, Zach."

We both laugh. His laugh makes me feel good and I greedily want to hear more. I don't think I am very good at flirting. I know I need to up my game with banter and innuendoes, but he hasn't run screaming yet, so I guess I am doing something right. I take a very large gulp of wine, swallowing it quickly, ensuring I don't choke on it again, and I feel it warm the back of my throat.

I am pleased that it is starting to make me feel more relaxed, calmer, and more confident without stuttering or making too much of a fool of myself. He leans in a little closer to me and I feel his warm beer breath against my skin, which makes me close my eyes briefly and shudder in delight.

Am I supposed to be this excited about a male?

"I hope you are impressed," he continues, "because you are smart, funny, well-travelled..." he pauses and looks me up and down, then gazes into my eyes. "And beautiful."

Ah, that word again. *Beautiful.* It rolls off his tongue so easily that I might actually start to believe him. I stare at his perfect mouth and wonder how he would taste in mine. "Wow, you are full of compliments, aren't you?" He raises his eyebrows in mischief. "Yeah... I am impressed."

We both smile at each other. The chemistry oozes from us both and we continue chatting and flirting (very badly on my end). The minutes slide into an hour and I love how the conversation is easy.

Who knew we had so much in common?

And his voice is such a stunning, deep and soulful sound. To be honest, he could have recited Pythagoras' theorem, or the periodic table and I would have hung onto his every word. Maybe this birthday is turning out not so bad after all.

"I know this conversation is very forward, but would you like to grab some dinner with me? I know a great Thai restaurant not far from here."

I feel excitement radiate through my body. I have never been asked out for dinner, never truly been kissed by anyone apart from maybe Rupert last year on the sports field. And he definitely did not count – it was a dare, and it was like a washing machine exploding on my face. I think he missed my mouth completely and I had to wipe the saliva off with a tissue. I grimace slightly at that thought.

What was even worse was that he thought it was a good kiss. I mean, who makes that mistake? Was he even there?

"Like a date?" I semi-blurt out. He looks a little surprised, then thoughtful for a moment, then smirks, oh that smirk.

"Would you like it to be a date?" He looks deep into my eyes like he is trying to figure me out. He leans slightly forward again, initiating another shiver in my body, answering my question. "Yes, Cora, like a date."

Three

The meeting – Zach

I was having a quiet weekend to myself, so I decided to push my-self out of the normal routine of hiding in my house and went to the pub in town to drown out some of my melodramatic and melan-choly thoughts. And honestly, there was some anger there too, and beer was the only way to deal with my mood. I was having an utter bag-of-wank week, and sitting in the quiet pub for a few hours, drinking, made me feel like me again. Not that I have a drinking problem – at least I don't think I do – it was more of me being alone, me being me, just me. No one making demands, no papers to mark, no teenage kid drama from school, no home drama, just me, and I like it. I like it a lot.

I internally kick myself.

I should do this more often if this is all it takes to make me chill out and, whilst I think of it, take up a hobby. I need to make more of an effort to be an adult, socialise, and even make friends. I blow out a puff of air and sink lower into my seat. It has been several months since I made the move here, to this sleepy countryside town, and so far, it hasn't turned out too bad.

Maybe the anonymity helped.

When I decided to move, the city seemed too fast-paced for my liking and moving from County Antrim to this small town In England, near my aunt was perfect. No one knew me or my past. I was just the new guy with the hot accent (my aunt's words, not mine), and no one paid too much attention to me. No one knew my pain, and I liked it. The new start was refreshing, cathartic even. I could be anyone from anywhere. It made me want to look forward to the future, rather than having the daily reminders from people when I was back home, with their sad and pitiful faces.

I didn't want or need that.

Home. That isn't home anymore – this is my home.

I must stop looking back, I can't keep living in the past. I feel it takes a part of my soul every day and I need to be stronger; I have to be stronger; the new me starts today. I take another large gulp of my beer and my mind wanders to work. Work has been a good move, too, and people seem friendly, but I like to keep to myself, work hard, get in and get out. Not that it stopped the other single co-workers from trying to flirt when they heard I was single.

Don't get me wrong, I love the ladies, but I haven't met or seen anyone that is enough to tempt me, or half tempt me, either. What was it my dad used to say?

"Don't shit where you eat," which I thought was a stupid saying when I was younger, but I get it now.

Plus, I like to keep busy with my time, so really, in theory, I don't have time for any dating or shenanigans of any kind. I look around the pub and enjoy its rustic feel with its open fire and oaky smells. I have only been in this pub a few times, a wee bit out of my way from where I live, but that's a good thing. I am not here to socialise, make friends, or bump into anyone I know. I like the quiet; I like being on my own. I like minding my own business, which means you don't expect anything from people, and they don't expect anything from you.

Perfect.

But then *she* walks in, the girl-next-door type (you know, the one that is so beautiful, but doesn't even know it? Cliché, I know). When I see her, I want to kiss her right away. I wonder what her lips taste like, maybe cherry, with how she is sporting a deep red shade of lipstick. She made me feel like I want to take her down over the bar and touch her all over. Especially her boobs, they just seem perfect, not too big so they would get in the way, or too small, so I would need a map to find them, and I am already imagining what underwear she is wearing. Maybe red and lacy to go with those plump lips, or is she a silk lady? More importantly, what would she look like without anything on at all? Probably perfect, the way the fabric of that top and jeans cling to her curves. Or maybe just those black heels, with nothing else.

Oh yes! That is within five seconds of her walking in.

I blow out a shaky breath. I am turned on, but I am surprised by my body's reaction and thoughts. I like being alone, don't I? I am not looking for a girlfriend or a sleazy hook-up. I mean, it's been years, so maybe I should? Maybe that is why I am looking at her like a dog in heat. Or do I spend too much time with my best mate, right hand? I don't normally talk to women. I am not that guy. I am not a big talker generally, more of a suffer-in-silence type. But mostly, I have never really had the time in my life. But she, she made me want to make the time. She is something else. From across the bar, I can see her bright emerald green eyes and sun-kissed look.

She takes my breath away.

Thank goodness those bloody beers gave me enough courage to talk to her. Again, no drinking problem, I just like to let the steam off at the weekends... sometimes, when I get the chance, I am a busy boy.

Do I want to talk to her? No... Maybe... I have drunk too much and should go home.

Then I realise this huge inner monologue that is happening, and I am still staring at her. Which then made me feel a wee bit like a stalker, but she seemed so lost in her thoughts she did not even notice me.

That annoyed me, which again is surprising. Why am I feeling like this? Like a horny teenager all over again, unsure of those rollercoaster emotions, making me feel confused, definitely making my dick perk up, down, boy! I should talk to her, but what if she doesn't want to talk to me, though? Maybe I can get her to notice me, I can cough, or nudge her as I walk past, wow, this is very childish. But then she silently 'cheers' herself and starts muttering, which makes me laugh. Without warning, verbal diarrhoea falls out of my mouth and I ask her what she is celebrating.

She intrigues me.

It starts off a bit cheesy, and my flirting skills are a bit rusty, or non-existent, but she doesn't seem to mind. She seems a wee bit shy but intelligent, and now I am closer to her, she is even more beautiful, and her smile, wow, it's like sunshine. I may just cum on the spot. She is damn right the sexiest woman I have ever seen. After only a few minutes of speaking with her, the thoughts of kissing her seem to intensify.

Would she think it weird if I just grab her and start caressing her? Luckily, she throws her drink over me, which snaps me out of my dirty thoughts. Otherwise, I would have had to have gone to the toilet and re-adjusted my pants.

Man, I haven't felt this horny in... ever. I see she is checking me out, yeah, I work out. I look my best at the moment, daily running and those weights I purchased on *Amazon* last year have done their job.

I feel the chemistry flowing between us, and I know she feels it too. Then she tells me she is studying music at university, and her passion for it just lights up her face. This girl is perfect for me.

Where did that come from?

It scares me how easily she has drawn me in after only knowing each other for a few minutes. Okay, she has stopped talking. I need to get to know her better. This is the first time I have connected to someone like this since... I can't even remember. I have to ask her out, to know who this mysterious girl is, even if I only have her for one night.

This is going against all of the rules I have set for myself. I told myself I wanted to be alone and that I didn't need anyone. I wouldn't need anyone ever again. But maybe, just maybe, she is a sign that it is okay to be open to someone new, to someone different, who could make me laugh and maybe I didn't have to do this alone anymore. I know it's forward, but I lace my hands through hers and feel her warm, soft hands in mine. What would it be like to have her hands over my pants or, even better, in them? I make the quick suggestion of food before I make a fool of myself. I want to kiss her as we walk to the Thai restaurant around the corner. It took a whole minute to pep talk myself into it and then I think, fuck it; I grab her close and kiss her softly on the mouth.

Four

The kiss —Cora

H is lips feel so warm and soft against mine. The kiss comes as a surprise, but it's definitely welcome. I stand a bit rigid at first, unsure how to react, but he pulls me closer and glides his hands up the arm of my coat and holds his cool hand upon my cheek, rubbing it softly with his calloused thumb. I suck a breath in, and the smell of mint and citrus overtakes my nose – his smell. I start to relax a little more, closing my eyes, enjoying the feeling, trying not to think about this too much and enjoying being wanted.

And he kissed me first!

I move my hands through his hair and a wave of excitement hits me as he parts his lips further and pushes his tongue gently into my mouth. A small involuntary moan escapes my mouth. Now I am enjoying this. He is an excellent kisser, soft but dominant and his tongue strokes inside my mouth perfectly. Rupert's washing-machine kiss can go shove it. This is the kiss I have been waiting for, the fairy tale kiss, where everyone lives happily ever after. If he is this good at kissing, I bet he's great with his hands...in my knickers!

Shite, I haven't shaved, he definitely can't put his hands in my knickers!

He tastes like beer, I can't say I have ever liked that taste, but I think it's my new favourite flavour on him. His kiss is intoxicating. I want more. I want him closer. He moves his lips away from my mouth and kisses me gently down my neck which makes me shiver in excitement. My breathing is becoming hot and heavy. I feel I can't get enough air in my lungs, but I love this feeling. He breathes softly in my ear, whispering.

"I have been imagining kissing you from the moment you walked into that pub." He nibbles gently behind my ear. Who knew that was a turn-on?

"And?" I respond breathlessly.

"Reality is so much better."

He seals another kiss on my mouth and he pulls me even closer. I feel dizzy with excitement. I begin to imagine what his naked body would feel like against mine. His hands start to glide down my back and cup my arse. Then he grabs it. I jump a little and he lets out a little chuckle. I feel breathless and sexy. I start to feel this may escalate further and I slightly panic.

Do I want my first time to be down an alley?

That is pretty disgusting, or maybe sexy, or even desperate. Zach being this close is clouding any coherent thinking. At that moment, his phone starts to ring. He freezes and curses against my lips, pulling away from me abruptly. Even when he curses, with his accent, it's still sexy. I wonder if he is into phone sex because I would pay to hear that accent! He answers his phone, walking a few steps away from me. I can feel how fast and wild my heart is beating and also how slightly aroused I am.

Scrap that. I am soaked.

Even though his voice is low, I can still hear his side of the conversation. His voice is soft, he doesn't sound mad even though his posture and his furrowed brows say otherwise.

"Yes… of course… I will be there right away… please do not worry… okay… bye." He looks back at me and seems guarded, and sad. He is nothing like the confident, sexy man that was with me a few moments ago. He sighs, "I have to go."

My stomach drops with disappointment, what was that phone call? He closes the distance between us and steals my breath with a quick and passionate kiss leaving me feeling greedy for more.

He pulls away and looks at me for a moment, unsure what to say. I try to hide the sadness on my face. I want him to ask me out, anything, but I am too chicken shite to say it.

Rejection is not my forte. I have had far too much of that in my life. And after the last 24 hours, I am not ready for any more.

"Right, bye, I guess?"

I didn't want to look at him, but knew he heard the disappointment in my voice. He steps away but speaks softly.

"I'm really glad we met..." he hesitates for a moment. "Can I give you my number?"

I nod, unsure of what to say. I hand over my mobile and he puts his number into the contact list, while I do a happy dance in my head.

He DOES want to see me again, OMG!

He places it back into my hand, holding his there for a few moments and gazes into my eyes, piercing into my soul. Or is this the look that says, giving me his number isn't the right thing to do? Then he is gone. Although I am confused by his parting look, I am excited at the possibility of seeing him again and resuming that mind-blowing kiss. I see a text has finally come in from my friend Sophie:

So, when ya meetin' me ho bag? Am at the square.

I've been gone 18 months, and nothing has changed. I need to see my friend now. We have so much to catch up on. I let out my little happy dance, this shitty day has turned into awesomeness. I trot back to the square; this psychotic smile isn't going anywhere.

I actually feel happier. It frightens me a little.

I hear Sophie before I see her as she squeals at me from across the square and gives me a big, suffocating hug like we haven't been apart for 18 months, more like 18 days. We've been friends since primary school, and we have semi-kept in touch since I left. She kept on saying she would come and see me, but she never did, which selfishly hurt a little, but it's not as if I just lived down the road anymore. She links her arm with mine and we walk back towards the high street up to the leisure centre. Apparently, there's a roller disco in the leisure centre hall today for 16-18s, and Sophie says it's all the rage in the town at the moment.

"You know you are over two hours late?"

"Shut up. I am not?" She looks me deadpan in the face. "I had a hair, face and then a wardrobe issue, these things take time." I roll my eyes at her. To be fair, she looks amazing, her hair is perfectly styled straight and her make-up is flawless. I thought I did a good job, but the smoky eye looks good on her. Her dress sense has always been something I loved and raged about.

Whatever she wore, she looked great. Even dressing down in skinny jeans, a crop top and a leather jacket, she was like a fashion queen.

"So, tell me all about the boys in the Middle East, are they as fit as they are here?"

"Are there fit ones here?"

"No," she scoffs "They're all boys, acting like stupid, little children, but think they are men," she huffs. "I need a university man or someone who is a millionaire and mature. I want to be taken care of."

"An easy find then," I mock.

"Obviously, I am not asking for much."

We laugh as we walk quickly up the street beside the canal. The high tree tops rustle, with the burnt winter leaves trying so desperately to hold onto the branches but the bitter wind rips them from their home and they fly free into the distance. *That sounds like a great start to a song*. The sun has almost set and we chat about school starting in a few days.

As we arrive at the leisure centre, I am grateful for the warmth again and go to pay the £5 entry fee to the leisure hall (which Sophie interjects and pays for whilst wishing me a happy birthday) and I pick out my correct size of roller skates. They smell like fusty, old spray, but I put them on and lace them up without an outward complaint. The lights are low with lots of disco balls and flashing lights. The room is busy and some chart music is playing. It looks super cheesy, but I like cheese, with extra cheese!

"You look so tanned Cee Cee… you've lost weight too."

"Thanks…" *I think.*

I follow Sophie onto the skating floor. I keep looking around in case I see Zach again, which is utterly ridiculous since he left to deal with whatever problem he had, and why would he even be here*?*

Brain, calm down. It was just a kiss. An AMAZING kiss.

I push his beautiful face to the back of my mind and Sophie and I skate around a few times. Despite not doing it for years, I am pleased I still know how to do it. I don't even fall on my bum! Sophie chats to a few other girls and boys as we skate around, and some make the odd conversation with me. I wasn't particularly in the 'cool' crowd before I left, or had lots of friends.

Sophie was my bestie, but then I sort of didn't make many more firm friends. I think some of Sophie's friends were polite to me, but they never went out of their way to make an effort, and to be honest, I was okay with that. I think living in a small town with my mum's past habits of being the town drunk, no one really liked to associate with my family. But one of the many things I love about Sophie is that she didn't care, so we became great friends very fast.

After a while, Sophie indicates to come off the skating floor to grab drinks and we find a quiet corner whilst sipping on some slushies.

"You still holding onto your virginity?" I nearly choke on my drink.

Wow, she really does just come out and say it as it is, but you know what, we can have these mature conversations and talk about sex and stuff now, right? Like buying your first tampon in the shop on your own, and you feel like you are going to drown in embarrassment (so much so that you can't even look the cashier in the eye because they might recognise you and tell everyone you know you've started your period) because apparently as a 13-year-old, it's the worst thing to happen to you, how naive I was back then. Now I couldn't care less.

"Yep, still got the V card, I am holding onto it, I am not giving it away, I want the whole deal, someone who gives a crap. I want the passion, the romance with the petals and the candles, the guy with not only brains but a fit body. I want my love story."

Sophie laughs. "I tell you now girl, he does not exist, especially in this small town. At this rate, you will be alone forever, like the old lady from the *Simpsons*, lobbing cats at anyone that walks past your house, screaming profanities at your neighbours."

"Rude, it's a big deal to me," she shrugs indifferently, "you've got to work up to it, you can't just jump right into it, that's like, like, paid sex...right? Wait, you sound like you know it all?"

She smirks at me. Talking about sex so openly feels weird to me. Don't get me wrong, I had romanticised every which way it would happen. A guy who respected me and treated me right. We would have beautiful music playing, and it would be a warm summer evening, with petals all over the floor and soft candles lighting up the room all over the surfaces.

It would be romantically off the charts. He would take me out on a date, he would say how beautiful I was. I know he is real and he is somewhere out there. Maybe it was Zach.

"You've had sex?" She stops drinking her slushed drink and looks at me.

"Why do you say it like it's a surprise?"

"No, no, it's not like that." I drink some of my drink and look thoughtfully at her.

"So...what was it like?"

"First time, it hurt a bit and was a bit quick."

"The first time?!" I almost choke out my drink.

She laughs. "We have a lot to catch up on, girl."

Apparently so.

Five

It's just another day in our paradise —Cora

When is it appropriate to text someone you have just met? I want to do it straight away, but my brain kept telling me off. So, I decide to wait the whole two days (which now, looking at my phone, seems so stupid, whoever created this rule is an utter tool bag) before I text, I don't want to seem desperate, even though I feel it. I feel out of control already, after one meeting. I think about the afternoon, every fabulous second of it, and slow it down to analyse every single detail. I remember all the kisses, all the looks, his hands all over me, the way he complimented me, his easy laugh, obsess much?

I can't think of anything else.

I want more, like a child wanting chocolate and then being free to take a look in the *Cadbury's* shop, only to be given one bar of chocolate and told they are not allowed another. I tried to troll him on social media, but I never got his last name. It wasn't a formal meeting or something from Victorian times where we would meet whilst strolling through the park on a warm summer's day, our eyes lock on each other, and he bows and I curtsy. "Good day, sir, I am Miss Wilkinson, but you may call me Cora."

Erm no!

So how do I even cyber-stalk someone I don't know? I try. I try scrolling through hundreds of Zachs, but no one comes up looking like him. I decide to admit defeat around 11 pm on Sunday and text him. I delete well over 100 different types of messages before I actually sent one. Satisfied that the task is done, I lie on my bed, dejected and restless, trying to sleep.

I wake up early for my first day back to school, a ball of depression and anxiety weighing me down in my stomach for yet another new start. I check my phone and nothing. The text delivery service shows that it hasn't even been read.

Disappointing.

I suppose it has been less than 8 hours since he received the text, and it was kinda late when I did it, even if it did take all weekend to design a perfect and witty text message:

Hi, it's Cora, was great to meet you, maybe we can do it again soon? X

Okay, I take it back, it wasn't *that* witty, but at least I didn't have verbal diarrhoea and say the kiss was the best kiss of my life. I think you're so hot I want your babies! I mean, I could have sent that, but then he would *never* text me back. No kiss in a text means friends, one kiss seems gentle, two kisses you are having a great time, and three kisses are too eager.

So, I went with the cool one kiss, trying to rein in the Cora crazy train. Maybe he gave me the wrong number and it was all just BS and he just wanted a quick hook-up. But it felt so real. Deep breaths, I can't let one afternoon with Mr Hottie ruin my mood or my life! Even so, I felt prickles of hurt that he was ignoring me.

I feel so needy.

Right, snap out of it, I need to go to school, so get in the car and drive. Let's do this!

Driving to school feels weird; it's my old school that I am going back to and I do not know how to feel. I see the turn-off for school and a sense of dread consumes me. I start to feel scared of what people might say. Will they remember me? Do I want them to remember me? It has been 18 months, so who knows? I remind myself that it's only two terms (if it does go to shite, then it's not that long) and then off I go to university. Ah crap, university. I need to sort that out, and soon. The deadline is in a few weeks, yet another move to look forward to. A sense of panic washes over me, only two terms and then it all changes again. It's like my feet aren't allowed to touch the ground, or as if life doesn't want me to call somewhere home for very long, it is disorientating. But on a positive note, super awesome Dad bought me a cute little second-hand Micra, so that was an amazing birthday present. However, getting used to driving on the correct side of the road is not so positive – but I am super grateful not to take the bus.

What is it with buses? Honestly, they hate me. They arrive early when I am almost at the bus stop, so drive straight past, the arses. Then you wait for the next one, 15 minutes, not bad, but then you end up waiting 25 minutes for the next bus if it even turns up, and the bus is packed and I always, always sit next to the person who stinks! Daisy moans all the way there about how Dad won't let her wear hardly any make-up to school, but I tell her just to put it all on and hide from him during the school day. I mean, how hard is it to hide from your father, the headteacher? Then she continues to moan about how it's unfair that the 6th formers can wear what they want, but she has to wear the horrible, skirted uniform. As I make the turn into the car park, fighting the urge not to push my sister out of the car whilst still driving, I pull up and leave the car running to bask in the last few minutes of being in the bubble of my car. Daisy makes a swift exit from the car (thank goodness), hiking her skirt up and brushing her hair as she walks across the car park with such confidence, through the front entrance without even saying thank you (rude) and I sit, taking a deep breath.

I have that feeling of turning up late to a party or dinner and not knowing what to expect but turning the word 'party' and changing it to 'school.' I am the new kid once again. I check my phone as I wait for Sophie and see a text from Dad:

Good luck on your first day back, don't break the birthday present, Dad XXXXX

Same to you, see you soon! Cee Cee xxxxx

There's a sense of desperation in the air after the Christmas holidays, like everyone has a duty to be miserable (because we saved it all up in December and spent all our happiness at Christmas), including the weather, and trying to extract any fun out of January was going to be a low score. Luckily, I do not have to wait long for Sophie, which pulls me out of my melancholy thoughts. She promises to keep me close, which is reassuring as we set off for first period, English.

The school has not changed much; 6th form is a little different, with many posters saying don't do drugs and have safe sex. Standard. The building is four stories, something built back in the '90s with its brick walls that are made up of mini stones on the outside. The white windows are crusting around the edges and the inside isn't much better. The top half of the walls is deep orange, and the bottom half is deep blue.

Who paints these walls?

And more importantly, someone needs to sort out a colour match scheme, it is awful. The toilets aren't much better, with no toilet seats, a debatable locking system and graffiti of profanities scrawled everywhere. They don't stink of smoke with people vaping, it just smells like colourful rainbows in there now, and how they don't get caught is beyond me.

My locker is on the bottom floor, which sucks, as everything is on the other side of the building. I am bringing a backpack tomorrow; I don't care if it isn't cool.

English goes off without a hitch and not too much staring, which I am grateful for. We are studying *Shakespeare's Romeo and Juliet*, which is my all-time favourite. The film with *Leonardo DiCaprio* and *Claire Danes* changed my whole thinking of Shakespeare being dry. It really brought out the modern era of film, and when Dad took me a few years back to the *Royal Shakespeare Theatre* at Stratford-Upon-Avon, I almost shit myself with excitement. I fell in love with all the actors, especially Romeo. The theatre was so intimate I felt I was right there experiencing every moment with them on the stage. The bell goes to indicate the end of the lesson.

"Ready for music?" I ask Sophie.

"Yeah, I guess."

"Where's your can-do attitude?"

"She left long ago!" Sophie replies with a roll of her eyes.

The room hasn't changed much, still white-painted bricks, a long row of tables with keyboards on them, a side recording studio and a smell I can never quite place, like body odour and rust. I think this is my favourite room, not because of the smell but because I have so many fond memories of learning music here, and a wash of nostalgia hits me.

I feel I am now starting to relax, that I can settle back down and be okay here. I sit down in the only empty plastic seat and position the keyboard in front of me, unsure what the seating arrangements are and not wanting to piss anyone off. I start flicking through the music books and syllabus. Sophie is sitting with someone else at the back of the room, I guess her sticking to my side all day isn't going to happen. I look up and I swear I stop breathing because in walks Zach. My stomach drops like I'm on the tallest rollercoaster at a theme park and I am unsure whether to laugh or vomit.

Is there anywhere to hide in the music room? Of course, there isn't. Would it be odd if I just hide under the table?

He doesn't see me right away, because I keep my head down for the first few minutes and busy myself with the books to give myself a minute not to. Die. Right. Here. But when I peek up, he is looking at my face in a thunderous way, a look of horror and surprise very clear on his face.

Great, I made out with my teacher.

What the hell! I am in hell, if not then I am going to hell for this. That is my teacher. There are a lot of swear words going off in my head like fireworks, so it's kinda hard to pick a good one or any of them. It is all mixed together like the biggest word I know: supercalifragilisticexpialidocious and then shoved together as a very long swear word.

Deep breaths, Cora. This is literally unbelievable.

I close my eyes, take a few deep breaths and thankfully, a wave of calm hits me and all I can think of is I have kissed my teacher and it really doesn't matter now that he hasn't texted me back, he cannot hide anymore.

He. Is. Here.

Is this even my life right now? I open my eyes to see him still staring and I flash him a quick smile, (maybe two thumbs up) he recovers quickly from his shock and I subtly glance around the room to see if anyone has noticed this interaction. Some of the pupils are side-glancing at me, but not at Zach. They are trying to figure out who I am or remember my face.

Crap.

Hopefully not about the past we desperately ran away from. Please do not remember why I left... Zach clears his throat and pastes a professional smile on his face. Once he started talking, I couldn't pull my eyes away from his perfect face, like a moth to a flame.

"Good morning, class, I hope you all had a great Christmas holiday?" No one verbally responds except a few students who nod in acknowledgement. He shuffles some papers on his desk and continues, "from the paperwork on my desk, it seems Cora is joining us back from the... UAE... it says you attended here before?"

He looks at me, eyebrows raised, and I just cannot get any words out. My mouth is dry and if I try to speak to him, I am sure it will come out as some sort of high pitch gibberish. I see a million emotions wash over his face, so I nod, trying to look cool, even though I am sure I just vomited in my mouth and swallowed it. "Great," he continues. "I am sure everyone remembers you." He looks a bit shocked and adds, "Because you have been here before." He clears his throat again, switches on his laptop and pulls up a PowerPoint. "I have emailed everyone the deadlines for your A-level examination, for the music piece and your written work, so no exceptions on lateness, blah blah blah..."

I cannot even listen to him. I want to run, run far, far away, I finally meet someone whom I like and he seemed to like me annnnnnnnnd he is my teacher. What kind of messed-up universe is this? I thought coming back home meant I was being swept away from the drama, but nope, it would seem I have run right back into the thick of it.

"...don't worry we are all in this together, I will arrange small tutor groups this week so we can work together on what piece you want to submit, so does everyone know what they need to do?" In my internal breakdown, I notice that he does not even look at me, a class of 15 pupils and he does not even look at me during his 10-minute speech/rant, staring at everyone in the class but me.

Damn it!

I can't look away from this car crash of a disaster, my, eyes, will, not, look, away! He's painfully obvious about ignoring me.

"Yes, Mr Jones." Some of the other students' chorus. Jones, so now I can officially socially stalk him, Zach Jones, I am onto you, or on you, or under you, well, that is even better. I smile smugly to myself. I wonder what he looks like under that fitted shirt and deep red tie. He looks mighty sexy, oh yeah. Closing my eyes and visualising back at the pub, he takes off his shirt slowly, revealing a toned chest, all sweaty. I lick my lips with anticipation.

"Cora?" I snap open my eyes and refocus. Mr Zach Jones smiles patiently with a voice that has a devastatingly neutral tone. A total turn from a few days ago, with his sexy whispers and flirtations. I shudder, does the room feel colder? "Do you know what piece of music you want to perform?" I nod again, still not ready for those vocal cords to make an appearance.

After a two-hour gruelling process of trying to stay focused on the piece of music on my keyboard – thank goodness for headphones – I hear the bell go. Stefan, the most sort-after boy in the school, swaggers over to me and looks me up and down as if deliberately taking his time to check me out. As much as I am sure some people would be impressed by this kind of attention, I inwardly want to vomit.

I quickly glance over at Zach, who is talking with another student, we lock eyes briefly, but he looks away: *now* you look. Sophie is behind him, putting stuff in her bag and waggles her eyebrows in recognition.

"So, ya back?" I pull off my headphones and start putting away my equipment.

"Looks like it," I respond, not really wanting to engage in this when I am on a mission impossible. I need to talk to Zach now. Stefan nods.

"Cool," he pauses, and I look at him. "Nice dress."

"Erm, thanks?"

"Makes your boobs look bigger." He gives a cheeky wide smile as if he has just complimented me. I roll my eyes a little.

"Okay."

"See you around." With that, he leaves the classroom.

I don't know what to make of that, but at least it wasn't 'your mum's a druggy' or something. Maybe people have 'forgotten' about my past.

"You coming?" Sophie calls at me from the door. I make an excuse that I need to talk about the exam to

Mr Jones. "Will meet you in the common room then?"

I nod enthusiastically and wait until everyone has filtered out, pleased this is a double period and now there's a short break for lunch. I walk over, but he continues to shuffle papers like he's super busy and is looking rather nervous, which is cute, but right back atcha. I am ready to poop my pants.

"Zach..." He stops what he is doing and flinches a little.

Ow, a cold reaction. He sits down behind his desk to keep the distance between us. Is that the 'stay back because I can't control myself' vibe or is it the 'I don't want anything to do with you' vibe?

"Cora... I... do not know what to say." He sighs and shakes his head a little.

"I am surprised at the," I wave my hand around, "the situation as you are..."

He scoffs a little. "I think that is a little bit of an understatement," he responds coolly, avoiding eye contact. Neither of us says anything, silence, not good.

"I had a really good time the other day... with you." Lame response but we have to start somewhere.

"You need to understand, that the other night was..."

"Amazing." I interrupt, I don't want him to say he regrets this. That kiss was unforgettable, not regrettable. I see his face twitch like he wants to smile, and his eyes start to roam my body as in some sort of remembrance.

Take it in, just look at me.

But he regains his solemn face quickly like he cannot break character and takes a glance towards the door blowing out air from his mouth in frustration.

"I got carried away, I didn't know you… went here, you said you were at university."

"You assumed."

"Right…" disappointment covers his face as if I lied to him on purpose. Maybe I did, a little. He shakes his head and runs a hand through his hair. I can see that he is not happy. "Even so, I am your teacher. You are my student. This is, was, an unprofessional line to cross."

"What line did we cross? That we both have a lot in common, that we enjoyed each other's company, we are both consenting adults here, Zach-"

"-Mr Jones," he interrupts.

Ouch.

His cold words sting again, and his teacher barrier is up. He sees the hurt reaction on my face and his face softens.

"Look, I am serious. Please, forget this ever happened, I could lose my job over this." Leaning over the desk, I place my hand softly over his, hearing him take a sharp breath in, whilst his eyes dip down to witness my hand entangled over his. The desire to touch his face is unbelievable and I wet my lips unconsciously just thinking of those soft and urgent kisses he gave me a few days before. Why does he have to be so hot, a great kisser and a good guy with morals?

"I can't deny we had an instant connection, and I know you felt it too. We could be something if you just give us a try."

"Us, there is no us," he replies coldly. He realises my hand is still covering his and he pulls his hand away from mine. He stands up from his desk so that there is even more space between us. He pauses before he responds and looks at me, his face unreadable. "Whatever I feel, felt. It has to stop, now."

"Why? Nobody knows... nobody has to know." I start to walk around the desk and he backs away further.

"This is not appropriate, and I think it is best you leave my class." He takes a deep breath and stares into my eyes, he looks helpless. "Please," he whispers. I stare at him for a few moments. Ah, those puppy eyes, dang it, he is good. So, I turn to leave his class, defeated and feeling he has won, for now. I try not to hate him when I see the relief on his face as I leave the room, that he doesn't have to deal with me anymore. But one thing he doesn't know about me is that I am persistent and, when I want to be, patient.

Six

Another one bites the dust, Zachary Jones style!

W ell, fuck my life, I did not see that one coming! I have no words.

Seven

The broken promise –Cora

I t had been a few days since the first encounter with 'Mr Jones' and to be honest, those days have been a bit of a downer. I had an uncontrollable urge to text or even call the first day, which I had to talk myself down from, mostly every hour, and distract myself, *a lot*. I spent many hours trying to cyber-stalk him, again, now that I knew his surname, but jeez, he is good at being undiscoverable. Apparently (according to the internet) he does not exist, or he hates the internet, which I just find odd for this day and age of being so connected, but each to their own. Then, I felt angry and the thought of storming into his room and demanding a better explanation, crossed my mind many times, felt more justified.

I must have written more than a thousand text messages and sent zero. I didn't know whether it was still because of those pleading eyes to stay away, or that I was a chicken and scared of rejection. The non-text, the radio silence, I did not know what was worse. But then my rational non-teenage brain materialised and talked sense into my thoughts (even though my lusty heart was screaming out for him). I realised it was all irrational thinking, and I knew better than to compromise his job. He seemed so vulnerable and sad, the way he said please with those eyes.

How could I be so demanding? How could I say no to him and his beautiful face?

That beautiful face!

I knew I had to stay away because, yes, it was wrong to be so attracted to my teacher, but I didn't know he was my teacher when we first met, so does that make it okay? Even so, I have to stay away. However, the next day I found myself taking the long route to English and Media Studies just to walk past the Music block, slowly walking by. I even loitered a few times, pretending I was waiting for Sophie, but I never saw him. It seemed like he was being quite successful at avoiding me, which was even more frustrating. By the third morning, I was feeling super depressed, and my hormones flooded in like a beast. I cried into my pillow that morning and hated on life. Even the fantasies of Zach were becoming unwelcome in my head.

I just want the real deal. I want more of him.

I couldn't even pull myself out of bed on time. Daisy and I were late for school. She stole my make-up, so we ended up arguing in the car and she made me so angry I drove straight over a mini roundabout without looking and I nearly crashed. I pulled over onto the curb to calm down and we soon made up to talking levels after that. Who knew nearly crashing the car would make my sister nice to me?

However, a school email came through from Mr Jones and my heart almost stopped, but it was a disappointing read, cc'd into Stefan Routledge, subject: Music A-levels, and a short message about joint tutor time today at 2 pm. I swear, after that message, time slowed down, and the minutes felt like forever until I got to see him again. The waiting was excruciating, I didn't even try to hide it. Even Sophie noticed me staring at the clock willfully in each lesson and started asking questions. I told her I had irritable bowel, and she didn't say a word after that. Finally, at almost 2 pm, I detour to the toilet, apply some lip gloss and stare at my reflection. It doesn't particularly cheer me up, but my foundation has covered any blemishes I had this morning, and my girls are looking super perky in this V-neck dress.

I arrive a few minutes early, hoping to talk to him, or anything really before Stefan arrives, but to no such luck. It seems he is running over from the last session.

Convenient.

Eventually, a few other students from my music lesson come out, and okay, here goes nothing. I push open the thick, wooden red door and stroll in casually, my heart beating a million times a minute. Wearing a shorter than normal dress, a bit tighter on the top to show off my assets but not too short that Dad would complain. However, I look good. I took my time this morning when getting dressed, (despite being late) maybe, psychically, I knew I would see him today. My mouth feels dry, sweaty pits and hands are not a good look for me – hormones get lost.

Breathe Cora.

He looks up and flashes his cute, dimpled smile. My stomach flips. That smile is enough to make my legs wobble and combust on the spot into a puddle of mess. I could just strip him naked and play out the scene where the papers get thrown everywhere, and things smash over the floor, but we don't care. We give into our desires, we make love over the desk amid the passion and pure lust, and nothing stands in the way... well, in films, it happens that way. In the films, the girl always gets the boy.

Bloody films.

"Hi Cora, take a seat."

Ah. The formal approach. No sex or making out on the desk, disappointing.

I discreetly push the door closed; grateful it works as I see it click shut. Zach has not noticed and no sign of Stefan.

Fabulous.

"Yes, Mr Jones." I sit on one of the hard, plastic chairs on the other side of the desk and wait. He watches as I do this, with his sexy furrowed eyebrows, like something is troubling him. I hope it is me. I hope it is my short dress and my perky breasts. We stare at each other momentarily, and I see his eyes flit quickly over my dress.

I look good and you know it.

He clears his throat, "How have you been settling back into school?"

"Why? Are you worried about me?" I try to throw my best flirtatious smile, but it probably came out as a grimace. I may need to practise this in front of a mirror later.

The smouldering look by Cora! He raises his eyebrows, "I like to check in with all my students." I am struck down again, although I notice his voice is a little high-pitched.

"No Stefan?" I try to change the subject.

"Clearly not," he looks disappointed that he has not yet turned up. Yet another burn. I stand abruptly and he seems taken back.

"Shall we reschedule then, Mr Jones? I don't want to be *inappropriate* in your classroom." Well, that came out cattier than I intended, but damn did it make me feel good! In his stupid, beautiful face, two can play this game, check mate! He contemplates the words for a moment. I take my bag and begin to make my way to the door.

"Cora, please, sit down. This is ridiculous." I stop and turn to look at him.

You're ridiculous!

He gives me a long, hard look – well, hello, sexy, serious face – and the tension in the room is thick. I am sure I could slice some of it with a knife and eat it like cake.

"Is it? I really am unsure if you can be my teacher when I know what we have done together and when I feel like *this* towards you."

"I have absolutely no idea what you are talking about."

I hang my head in defeat. "Yes, yes you do," I whisper. The silence in the room is deafening. He hesitates for a moment, then walks over and stands close to me. His cologne consumes me. His smell of mint and citrus is absolutely intoxicating. The urge to take off his shirt and tie and lick his face flickers across my mind, again. I internally smile and silently groan.

Why is it when he is this close that all my thoughts turn to this: sex, kissing, more sex – stay strong Cora. I can do this, stay strong.

He looks at me with determination, but before he speaks, a small lock of hair falls around his face and without hesitation, I brush it back with the tip of my fingers and tuck it behind his ear.

He closes his eyes briefly and I pause for a moment... ah what the hell, I am already touching him. I trail my fingers down his clean-shaven face, his breath hitches and his dark eyes open full of lust.

Ah, there he is, my Zach. I missed you.

I feel the sparks burning between us and while there was a lot of tension in the room a moment ago, it is now quickly turning to burning desire. He takes my hand slowly away from his face and holds it in his as his thumb gently rubs the back of my hand. Such a simple gesture, yet so romantic. I feel a warm tingle up my arm, the sexual chemistry radiates between us just like it did when we first met, and I know he can feel it too. It is written all over his god-like face. He cautiously steps closer and I feel his warm breath on my face. He bites his lower lip a little as I stare into his eyes. I could get lost in those brown mysterious eyes, so beautiful. I lift my head slightly, so ready for the kiss, ready for him. My heart is beating wildly, so loud, maybe he can hear it?

His hand gently cups my cheek, and I lean into his warmth. Suddenly, I hear voices outside the room, and he drops his hand from mine. I feel the loss immediately. He gestures for me to sit. I do as he says, sad that the moment has passed. He sits on the other side of the desk. He sighs and we sit in silence for what seems like forever, but then he whispers.

"I meant what I said the other day by crossing the line, I can't do anything like this… I can't, this position that we have been put in, does not just affect me."

"Who are you trying to convince, me or you? Because I know how I feel about you."

He stares at me for a few moments as if taking me in, as if he is actually hearing me. He is just about to respond when Stefan comes barging into the room.

Stefan, you arse!

"Soz teach, the bus was late. Oh hey, Cora," I scowl over at him, trying to kill him with my angry and disappointed eyes, but Zach seems to sigh with relief that the conversation had to end and smiles at him appreciatively. He is not getting out of it that easily. I know you like me; I just do not understand why you are fighting so hard against this. Yes, this is forbidden. Yes, this could get us into a whole load of trouble, but he is worth it. I have never felt like this about anyone in my whole life. He is my one, I just know it – I will crack him like a tough nut.

"Not a problem. My last tutor group overran, and we have only just sat down."

I force a smile, even though I feel that I want to punch Stefan in his whole face for turning up and not letting me continue my conversation with Mr Hottie. I sit through 30 minutes of information on how long the composition should be (not less than 4 ½ minutes), and that the direct exam time will be with Zach. He will supervise to show the authenticity of the song. I will need written examples of past songs. A performance and briefs from past exams. I will need to compose a melody, but it should only last around 10 minutes for the first exam. After writing my name down for piano, I start to imagine what it would be like to take Mr Jones over the desk again with some one-on-one, naked time! I wonder what would have happened if Stefan hadn't walked in, and if Zach would have slowly leant over and kissed me softly on my lips. He would whisper that he couldn't stay away from me any longer and demand that I be his. I cross my legs and squeeze my thighs; he makes me so frustrated, in more ways than one.

This is when I notice I can see Zach's legs under the desk, and with the position of his chair, Stefan cannot see underneath the desk. I stretch my leg ever so slightly, remove my heel and slowly move the tip of my foot up his leg. I see his jaw clench tightly, but he continues without missing a beat.

Sweetly done, if I say so myself. It's a bold move, but I am feeling desperate, my toe lightly glides up his leg, up to his knee, going a little higher to the good stuff. But he moves his leg away from me.

Boring!

As the tutor time wraps up, Stefan turns to me.

"Now you are back, Cora, maybe you'd like to come and see my band on Friday night, we are playing at the Basement Bar in town," he thrusts a flyer from his bag into my hand. "You should come, my number is on there, text me." He stares at my boobs blatantly for a moment and then he stands up and leaves the room, not waiting for an answer. Now, why can't Zach just blatantly check me out like that? But I am starting to understand that it is Zach's subtle movements I look for, like now, he looks bewildered and annoyed, with his sexy brows all furrowed. Well, thank you, Stefan, not so much of an arse now if you can make Zach cranky. The next tutor group is making their way in and, I get up to leave. My sister turns up at the door.

"Cee Cee, I need to speak with you!" She ogles at Zach as if she cannot believe how beautiful he is either. I walk towards her.

"What's up?"

"Is that your music teacher? He's well fit." I shush her, shoot Zach a small smile, and usher her out the door.

He definitely heard that, my sister has no filter, and it makes me feel slightly uncomfortable because Daisy isn't the first person to leer at him. And honestly, Zach doesn't seem to notice, he is either blind or immune to it. Looking back, he has a group of girls chatting at his desk. They're laughing loudly at something and trying to be near him, flicking their hair back and using ways to accentuate their breasts.

I huff as I have no claim over him. I should not be jealous when I was trying to do the same only moments ago. And yet, it seems that all I am channelling now is jealousy and rage.

"What do you want, Daisy?" I ask her crossly as she pulls her eyes away from Zach.

"I need a lift home." I look at her annoyed. "Cee Cee I've bled through my pants and my jumper is covering a nasty stain, I need to go home and change, don't be a bitch."

"You really know how to get to the point, don't you?" I sigh, "Come on, I'll take you home."

Eight

Still no words – Zach

It had now been a few weeks since that day when I walked into my classroom and there she was, the beautiful Cora from the pub. To say I was surprised was an understatement. Yet, she who had been my perfect sign that my heart was ready to open up again to new people, that my luck was meant to change, that now was the time to move on, was a joke. That *wonderful* sign got a sledgehammer and smashed itself to pieces and then shat all over it too, with the two fingers 'fuck you' gesture. Just joking, you can't meet new people, your luck is crap, and you are not ready to open your heart.

Go wallow in self-pity and be done with it!

She was my student, of all people she could be in my life, and she was that. I have to say that since that discovery, I have been feeling a bit low, a wee bit reserved. Going to work seems like a struggle. I want to see her, I want this to be okay, but it's all kinds of wrong. The conflicting messages my brain sends are making me feel all over the place. It is taking all of my efforts to avoid her as much as possible. I try not to look at her at all during class time and by the end of the lesson, I either leave the room or make myself busy with other students or teachers so that she would get the hint not to hang around and try to speak to me. To be fair, it is working, but I can see she is frustrated (when I dared to look).

I can't deny the attraction, even though this is 50 shades of fucked up, she is still a woman and I am still a man at the end of the day. And she is beautiful, another level beautiful, my kind of beautiful.

My Cora, *mine*.

And even those stolen moments of conversations in class, when asking her questions on the topic or her musical insight or knowledge, her replies are thoughtful and interesting. I try not to hang on to every word she says, or stare when she softly bites down on her lip when she is thinking of the right answer. And it makes me sadder, and madder that we cannot take this further, we aren't allowed to take this further. It is a constant battle in my head, day and night. I know it is wrong, I know it is unprofessional.

I know I will be fired; I know it all. Yet still, I want her.

I think of her, a lot, and when I lie in my bed at night, I think of her even more. It's hard, in my brain and in my pants. Yet, I am a big boy and an adult, and I know these life experiences are here to test me. And I can persevere. I can power through this lust, or whatever it is, because it can never go anywhere, *never, ever*.

A good pep talk, Zach.

Until we are alone, like today. When we are alone, my brain short-wires and thinks with its dick. It will not listen to reason and even though I am telling her with my mouth to stop, I am undressing her with my eyes. I want her to stay because I am selfish, and I need her to leave because this can never happen. Even when her fingertips lightly brush against my hair, it sends goosebumps all over my body and ignites my skin. It's like I am bewitched by her spell, bewitched by her. I nearly kissed her, I want to kiss her, and I am disappointed in myself that I stopped thinking rationally, again. But how long can I keep this up? It's as if we gravitate towards each other, and I mentally slap myself. It's a wake-up call that we cannot be alone. Otherwise, I may not be able to control myself, then what?

I could lose my bloody job.

Ten more weeks of teaching and then she will be gone, I don't know whether to feel relieved or sad that another person that I care about is leaving my life. But I know it will be for the best.

Only ten weeks Zach. That's all it is. You can ride this messy train.

What makes it worse is that her dad, my boss, is so nice. What would he think if he knew I wanted to sex up his daughter, that I had already stuck my tongue down her throat and that I wanted to stick my tongue in more places too. I often feel guilty and disgusted with myself when I speak with him about work or when we are in meetings because if he knew half the things I wanted to do to his daughter, I would be fired on the spot.

Maybe even sent to jail.

What the fuck is wrong with me? There are millions of women out there and yet the one I want, the one fate sends me, I cannot have. Why can I not move past this?

I have found myself drinking more in the evening, which is not like me. I feel I am regressing back to when things were bad before. Not even my daily runs are helping with my dirty thoughts and pent-up frustration. No matter how far or long I run. It helps clear my head whilst running and for those few minutes after, but I guess at this moment, I will take any break I can from thinking about Cora. It's times like these that I wish I had made more of an effort to make friends. Then I could rationalise this constant struggle, that someone could tell me to grow the fuck up.

Well, Zachary Jones, grow the fuck up!

Nine

The sleepover with Sophie – Cora

The next evening, Sophie invites me to stay at her parents' house. They are away for the week for their 20th wedding anniversary and we make plans for a sleepover. We sit and watch an old-school musical, *'Moulin Rouge,'* whilst singing along and eating popcorn. She grabs some alcohol from the cupboard and makes some Mojito-style drinks and refills some of the bottles with water, claiming that her parents won't even notice, which makes me laugh. I did offer to buy some alcohol (now that I am of legal age, oh I love saying that out loud), but apparently, I shouldn't bother when it's free from her parents' stash.

"I don't care how old Ewan McGregor is, I'd still shag him," I confess whilst watching the Elephant Medley part, my favourite bit. They both fall in love despite their differences. Even the London Musical of this was on point.

"Ewwwwww, serious?"

"Yes! A man who can sing, dance, is good-looking and the Scottish accent, what's not to love."

"I see your tastes haven't changed," she pauses for a moment. "What do you think of Mr Jones?" I try to act casual although I think that my heart has just hammered up a million times. Has she noticed me staring or him staring at me? Is it obvious that I stare into space in that lesson, listening to his voice and fantasising about him in any way I can?

"What do you mean?" I ask, trying to keep my voice as even as possible and not daring to look into her eyes, and play with the hem of her bedspread.

"Well, he fits the criteria, older, accent, musical. I would have thought you would dribble at him a bit. I mean, he is gorgeous, with a capital G."

"Yeah, I guess. I hadn't really noticed," I confess casually.

"Bullshit, everyone notices!" She eyes me wearily. "Wait! I know why... are you seeing someone?" I swear I nearly projectile vomit. I thought she was going to say she knew. I laugh nervously.

"Yeah, sort of."

"Okay, spill."

"Erm..." okay, lying to my friend isn't what I want, but I have to say something. Sometimes I hate the way she can read my emotions like an open book, "It's complicated."

"Complicated, how? Older?" I nod. "Wow, okay, why complicated? OMG, he's married and has kids, hasn't he?" My eyes bulge. "It is, I am right? Jeez, Cee Cee, what you went and got yourself in for?"

Well, that was it, the dam bursts and I start ugly crying. She hugs me. "How bad is it?" she asks, holding me and rubbing my back. I have had to keep the meeting with Mr Hottie in for so long, and even though I can't tell her the whole truth I can tell her everything else. So, I recount the whole meeting and then replace school with seeing him out in public and replace other bits of school with his wife and how he doesn't know what he wants. She sits there stunned for a moment or two.

"Well, there are two things we need to do now, we need to go out and get crazy drunk tomorrow night at Stefan's gig and dress you up and show you how amazing you are. We need to up your game."

"Up my game?"

"Yeah, you know, change your hairstyle, clothes, techniques. Show Mr Married Man how amazing you are and what he is missing out on."

"Right, and how do you suggest that?" She thinks for a moment and moves closer to me on the bed.

"Maybe your method was off?"

"My method?" I laugh dryly. "My method is fine."

"Show me," she insists.

"What? I am not showing you."

"Why? Show me and we can then see what you need to improve."

"Rude," I retort.

"It isn't, how are you supposed to get better at something if you don't practise." She had a point. "How many times have you snogged someone? Twice?"

"Three times, actually," as if saying that makes it any better. I haven't had the chance to practise or find anyone interesting enough to practise with.

"My case rests," she smirks smugly, whilst crossing her arms.

"Right, well, how many people have you snogged?"

"So many I have lost count... maybe, like, 30 or so..." I roll my eyes at her so far they nearly fall out the back of my head! "Close your eyes, pretend I am Mr Married Man and let's see."

"Sophie!"

"Cee Cee, come on, close your eyes." I feel like my head might explode with embarrassment, but I do as she says.

I let out a shaky breath and close them. I listen to my slow, light breath and then feel her close to me. She kisses me softly on my lips and I feel awkward. "Concentrate," she whispers. I imagine Zach and how we were in the alleyway and visualise me and him, again. I part my lips ready, and the kiss comes again, this time with a bit more power. I tilt my head to the side and move my hand to her hair. We move our lips together. She is really good at kissing, I open my mouth and invite her tongue into mine whilst doing the same to her, it is both sensual and intimate. We both pull back, bringing it to a natural stop and she looks at me and nods. "Not the technique, that was pretty good." I feel quite pleased with myself.

"Thanks."

"Right then, let's sort the hair and do a trial makeover! We need you out having a good time and forgetting stupid people."

"Soph... thank you..."

She nods again and starts rooting through her wardrobe as if we didn't just have a make-out session and it was the most normal thing to happen when popping over for a sleepover. This is why I missed her and love her so much; my best friend just takes everything in her stride and makes everything and everyone around her feel better about themselves and life.

She is definitely my person.

Ten

The Basement bar – Cora

Social teenage etiquette demands that on a Friday night, you have to be busy, going out, or, at least, had made plans, or life wasn't really worth talking about in your social circle at school. And the word on everyone's lips is Stefan's band. I decide to take Stefan up on his offer. So, Sophie and I head to town the next evening to watch the band play. Sophie's parents are still away, so we get ready at her house. She materialises with some cheap box of wine that tastes slightly like perfume and wee, but who am I to complain about free alcoholic drinks? I have zero money and even though I am over the legal age, I think Dad would explode his shite if he knew I was drinking like this. The fact that he let me go out tonight was a miracle. Sophie has spent the last hour on my face, with a smoky eye and some contouring that makes you look thinner, apparently. I have my hair in loose curls, and I look nice, really nice. I feel better about the 'Zach' situation and decide that it is time to grow up, a little, on this obsession with him and try to let loose and have a   bit   of fun.

"That's an unusual dress," Sophie comments, which is code for ugly. I throw her an unimpressed look. "Just wear my LBD and stop being a granny." I take off my flower-pattern dress and slip on her short black dress, which plunges front and back, leaving not much to the imagination. Sophie starts pulling my top together with tit tape; honestly, being groped by your friend is not how I envisaged the start of the evening. When she is finished, I stare at myself in the mirror.

"I look like a whore."

She smirks at me. "That's the plan! Here, wear my strappy sandals, they look nice with that dress. You know, for someone so beautiful, you are super awkward." I don't know what to say to that.

A few hours later, we rock up to the club, it looks like a dodgy back bar and a few people are vomiting outside. I look away in disgust, a group of men are leaving.

"Nice tits!" One of the men remarks as he walks by. I show him the middle finger.

"Get lost, idiot!" We enter and it does not get much better inside. The guys in there are circulating the room around the ladies dancing in the middle. It's like a cattle market and they're competing for the best drunken idiot in a five-mile radius. To be honest, many of them are coming pretty close, and the floor is unbelievably sticky. If I had worn my ballet pumps tonight, I think I would have lost both of my shoes already.

"This place is awful!" I shout over the music to Sophie.

"Yes, but for £2 shots, you can forget how crap this place is!" She roars with laughter.

"Quick, let's get a selfie." We pose and she tags us on social media.

The music is loud, it makes my ears ring, and the toilets are disgusting – when they had last been cleaned was anyone's guess. The toilets don't have any lids, which is such an odd concept, reminding me of school. The woman in the toilet keeps getting me to buy some rubbish in her basket like spray or lollipops, the drinks are full of sugar and most taste like the box of wine from earlier, but I have never felt so free in my life.

When Stefan and his band come on stage, the atmosphere changes and it turns into a brilliant night. I watch Stefan as he wildly jumps around the stage with his guitar, he looks good, and the band has promise. He walks around the stage as if he owns it and the crowd loves his band's edgy music. I see that he shoots me smiles every so often, which is cute, but I see other girls on the dancefloor shooting me daggers.

The dancefloor becomes busier as the night wears on, dancing close to Sophie, feeling free, I let the music take over. After a while, Sophie nudges me and I see several guys looking our way, I am liking this new attention. I think if I did this in the UAE, not only would Dad kill me, but the locals may do the same. The smoke machine streams through the air and I feel the drumming through my bones. This is what it is like to be a teenager, to drink, to dance like no one is watching, to laugh at stupid things and to wear very short dresses.

After several more songs and lots of crazy dancing, I am ready to sit down. My feet hurt and I need another drink. The band finishes up, and I clap and holler like a teenage fan, whistling as loudly as I can. So does everyone else. The band has gone down well with the crowd and I feel that this band will go far, they have the style, the good-looking guys, and the music is really good. After going to the toilet, I look around the dance floor for Sophie. She had eyed someone on the dance floor earlier and already has her tongue down his throat, fair play. It seems this time apart we have grown into different people. She used to be shy around boys and now she's filled out in all the right places and I think she threw shy as far away as possible. Now, she is confident and ballsy.

I like this new version of her.

Making my way to the bar, my head feels fuzzy and I feel happily tipsy. Sitting on the bar stool, I take off my heels and rub my feet. I think this is something I will need to get used to. The bar isn't too busy so I am served quickly and take a gulp of the alcopop.

I close my eyes, and I can't help but think of Zach, wondering what it would be like if he was here, was he thinking of me now? All of my thoughts are of him and they consume me. I cannot shake him; he has seeped into my skin and is holding me so hard I could cry. He was beyond beautiful, he was my obsession, and if only he would give me the time, I knew we could make this work. Just to hold him and kiss him again felt like such a faraway possibility. It made me ache with sadness. Why can't he just be with me? I know he likes me and I like him, but why can't things be simple?

I feel warm arms hold me from behind and I imagine it is Zach. He would kiss me and tell me how much he misses me. I lean into the hold and I feel a soft kiss on the side of my neck. I open my eyes in surprise; this is not Sophie. I turn and see Stefan's face. As much as he is easy on the eyes and has damp, sexy, floppy brown hair that clings to his forehead and long eyelashes that extenuate his baby blue eyes, he is just not Zach. Damn Zach. I think he has ruined me for all men.

Shite.

Stefan takes my moment of silence (or, in my head, a moment of weakness of not wanting to be alone) and leans in for a kiss and just for a second, I take it. I take the attention, I take the warm feeling that I am wanted, that I am pretty, and I kiss him back. I enjoy the soft kiss, but he shoves his tongue into my mouth too quickly – I am not ready for such an invading kiss. I think of Zach and the perfect kiss we shared.

How his kisses came in slow and sensual, and I welcomed him into my mouth without a second thought – this feels messy. I realise what a crappy person I am, I am thinking of Zach whilst kissing Stefan. I pull back. His kiss was nice, but the spark isn't there, not like it is with Zach.

"Stefan..." I whisper. "The thing is..." He looks a little stunned that I am going to say no, the arrogance just oozes off him. He flashes a cocky smile.

"What did you think of my band?" He swivels my chair so I am looking directly at him and his arms rest over me as if I have invited him to do so, closing me in so I can't escape. If this were a few weeks ago, I would have loved this. He likes me and he is cute, but again, not Zach. He still has that after-stage sweat and his eyes glow with excitement.

I smile. "You were great."

He frowns. "Great? How much have you drunk, Cora? We were bloody brilliant..." Sophie comes bouncing over with a huge smile on her face.

"You guys look sweet, I am going to go, you okay to get home by yourself?" She looks back at the guy she has been tongue-thrusting with for the last half hour. My stomach drops, great, dumped again. I muster up a smile.

"Sure, I'll grab an *Uber*." I stand up and sidestep Stefan, a perfect getaway.

"I'll take you, Cora. I drove tonight," Stefan chips in. Sophie starts to walk away.

"Fab, text me later." And she is gone. Double great. Stefan holds out his hand as if he expects me to take it. I hope he didn't see how disappointed I look or hear the biggest sigh that just came out of my mouth.

"Stefan, it's fine, I can get an *Uber*, not a problem."

"You will struggle to get an Uber; they're shit at taking orders back to our town as it's in the middle of nowhere. You know that. Let me just take you home, Cora, don't be weird." He walks to the stage, not expecting a response and grabs his guitar. Screaming more arrogance, he then says something to his friends, who look at me. So, did he say I am off to take Cora home or I'm going home to get some fun from Cora?

Ah, who cares, a free ride home.

I have to loosen up, and I have got pepper spray in my bag that Dad forced me to take before I left. I don't mind using that, either. I hate the way Dad sometimes treats me like the weaker sex, or that I should feel frightened to walk on my own. I know he only does it because he cares and to be honest, I might need it tonight.

The drive home is fast but quiet, as if Stefan can read my mood, which is great because I feel totally lost and crap about myself. Who kisses someone whilst thinking of someone else? Me, that's who! My whole body feels so confused, and just being a teenager is really confusing anyway.

One minute I am happy as a kite, laughing and everything. The next minute I am downing a tub of Cornish double-clotted ice cream crying into a tissue for no apparent reason. I also think Stefan needs driving lessons because he's driving like an idiot. He's going a lot faster than the speed limit, not even slowing down for corners and if we hit someone, I am not going to prison for his stupidity.

"Are you seeing anyone?" he asks. He doesn't take his eyes off the road, but the question surprises me. I wish, I want to say yes, but it would be a lie.

"Erm... not really," I reply.

"That sounds complicated."

I smile. "When did you get so intuitive?"

"I like complicated," he places his hand on my knee. That's not the first time I have heard that this week. I go to push his hand off my leg, but he holds my hand instead. He cannot take a hint, so I just let him hold it.

"Look, Stefan..."

"I can wait," he interrupts.

"What? I didn't say..."

"I like you, Cora, I can wait," he responds arrogantly *again*. Thank goodness we arrive at my house. He pulls into the double drive.

"You remember where I live?" I ask, confused.

"It's a small town." I pull my hand from his and unbuckle my seatbelt.

"Well, thanks for the lift."

"Cora?" I turn to look at Stefan, and he leans in and kisses me again. Damn, he is persistent, I gotta give him that. His kiss is soft, gentle and brief. Different to how it was back at the club. I enjoyed this one a little more despite having already told him no. He looks at me, waiting for me to say something. What does he want me to do or say? Fall at his feet and thank him for his kind words and that the kiss just changed my mind and my life? It's not that he is a rubbish kisser, it's just that I didn't want to kiss him in the first place. He seems nice, but he's a boy and Zach is the guy. I won't settle for a boy. I want the guy! He pulls back a little and looks at me, still waiting for me to respond, I give him a small smile, but I am now starting to get annoyed. He starts to play loosely with strands of my hair.

"So, what do I get for driving you home?"

He smiles cheekily and raises his eyebrows nodding down to his shorts. I look at him confused for a moment. Then it dawns on me that he wants me to play with his penis!

"You want me to wank you off?"

"You say it like it's a bad thing… you know, favour for a favour."

Now I am pissed. "I'm not a prostitute, Stefan!"

Exiting the car, confused about what just happened but glad to be home, I hear him say as I shut the door. "That's not what I heard." I am absolutely fuming now. I cannot get into my house quickly enough.

Eleven

The rehearsal – Cora

T he following week arrives, and Zach is still avoiding me like the plague. So, I settle into a routine of staring at him in lessons and going to my happy place. When I see him in the hallway around school, he still gives me butterflies. Sophie convinced me to come to the band's rehearsal this evening, which I did not want to go to. She gave me that pouty look with puppy-dog eyes that I could not say no to, but really, I think it's because she wants to snog Tash, the singer. She made me feel guilty about how I needed to be a good friend and support her. She doesn't want to go alone, looking like she's desperate. She said that Stefan was asking for me to come, how bad he is feeling for talking to me the way he did, and that I hurt his feelings by ignoring him.

I didn't want to be a bad friend, but the car experience with Stefan last week still left a bitter taste in my mouth.

This evening is an utter bust. The band spends the first half an hour seeing how many of them can burp the alphabet (it's disgusting). Stefan is throwing all his flirtations at me tonight and making the other bandmates snicker as if they're in on some stupid joke.

The dick probably told his friends he slept with me. All this male testosterone and peacocking to his friends makes me dizzy. I pretend I have a really important phone call and leave the room during a song so I can escape and have a breather. It's too much for me and he's starting to make me feel uncomfortable. The hints are not working. It's like he's never had a girl say no to him, which makes me laugh bitterly.

He's in for a real shock then.

I walk into the music room, hoping my favourite place will bring me enough strength to last the rest of the evening. Closing the door quietly behind me, I am surprised that the lights are on, but needing some space from all the ordeal, I close my eyes and lean against the door with relief. Maybe they won't notice that I left so I can go home. Stefan had tried to kiss me, again, trying to find any way to touch me or be near me. I even texted him the other day to say that I wasn't interested, and it was a mistake that we kissed, and can we just be friends?

I let out a sigh.

Should I feel flattered he likes me and is so persistent, or angry that he can't respect my boundaries? Stefan is cute and everything but Zach... I open my eyes and lock eyes with Zach, who's sitting at his desk. He jumps and snaps the book he's reading shut, knocking over his glass. He curses and bends from his chair to pick it up.

"Cora, what are you doing here? I... I... I didn't think anyone was up in the Music block tonight, it wasn't on the rota." His voice is slightly panicked as he mops up the spill, furrowing his perfectly shaped eyebrows.

Well, this evening just took an unexpected and amazing turn.

"Last minute band rehearsals, thought I would check it out, you?" He looks concerned as I approach his desk.

"Governor's meeting and my night off."

"Night off, a night off from what?" I approach the desk and see a half-empty bottle of whiskey, which is surprising, and I raise my eyebrows. "Tut, tut sir, no drinking on the job." I smile teasingly, but as I peer closer, his eyes are rimmed red as if he has been crying and his dishevelled hair and the loose tie confirm that my man is not happy. Jeez, he looks a bit of a sad mess. What new poop storm have I just entered? He shoves the bottle into his desk drawer, as if he has been caught underage smoking in the school toilets, and looks at me a bit sheepish. "Erm... is everything okay?" He looks away.

"Yep."

He answers a bit too quickly, and I'm not buying it. Something's not right. He sits back down and starts to read his book again as if I am not there. I pull the chair up next to him and sit in front with our knees touching. I take his book from his hands and put it on his desk and hold his hands in mine. He inhales at the touch, but any excuse to touch him.

"Mr Jones... Zach... is there anything I can do?"

He stifles a small laugh. "I am sat here, half drunk, a mess, and you are asking if there is anything you can do?" He lets out a big sigh.

"I care about you, of course I want to help." He smiles and I stroke my thumb over his hand, remembering how romantic and warm it made me feel a few weeks ago when he did it to me. I love it when he touches me. I desperately try not to take him into a bear hug and hold him close, telling him I am here for him, wanting his pain to disappear (and smell him a little – don't judge) and that I would do anything to see him smile. This raw emotion he's showing right now is damn right sexy as hell, and the penny drops.

I flipping love this guy, which really surprises and scares the crap out of me.

How can I be in love with my teacher? How can I be in love with someone I met three weeks ago? This is not good, not good at all, hormones suck! One intimate afternoon and several weeks of sexual tension, unrequited emotions, lots of side glances and a near kiss have sent me over the edge.

I need to get out more, but at least he hasn't pulled his hand away this time.

"You don't even know me, Cora," he whispers.

"That's only because you put this barrier up, I have to fill in the blanks, you won't let me know you properly. But what I do know, what I do see is a caring, disgustingly handsome, funny man that seems to have a lot on his shoulders." His mouth twitches a little and silence fills the air. He lets out another sigh, but this time he seems depleted. It hurts when he puts up the barrier. I know he is out of my league, an older, handsome man, who has a job, and I have an overactive imagination and live at home! His moods run hot and cold, or maybe he has just gone off me. I feel an 'I'm not good enough' panic start to arise.

"It's the second anniversary of my mum's death today, and I guess, I am just not dealing with it very well." I am unsure how to respond to that, Mum left Dad just after Daisy was born. She was in and out of our lives for years, us never knowing when she would turn up, her acting like she was never away, making more promises we knew she could never keep. Telling us how things were going to change and how much she loved us. She was always flaky and asking Dad for money and then, a few years ago, she was involved in a drink and drug scuffle and is spending the next five years in jail. That's when Dad snapped, and we moved away for a fresh start.

I know it's not the same for Zach.

He had someone he loved and then them dying on you. Whereas my situation, I never really knew my mum, always feeling let down, someone I never really counted on, and felt detached from, all I have ever really felt was guilt. Guilt for not being sad she wasn't there, guilt for not really missing her, because how can I be sad about something I've never had in the first place?

She made a choice and left us.

"Cora, it's broken me. Her death has broken me, and I don't know how to fix it. I don't know how to fix myself... it's been two years and I just thought it would be better by now, you know? It's as if I want to move on, but also, by doing that, I feel I am forgetting her." I nod, taking in a deep breath, I have no clue what to say, but he needs someone to listen to him. He's so vulnerable. A tear escapes from his eye and I brush it away with my thumb and cup his cheeks with my hands to make him look at me.

"You're not broken. You don't need fixing. You lost your mum, you are grieving."

Another silence, his gaze pierces me. "What about your dad?"

"Ah, yet another sob story. He died in combat when I was 14."

"Wow, that is sad. I never really knew my mum; she left us just after Daisy was born. She was in and out of our lives. She was not someone we could count on or look up to. But the loss is still there – I know it's not the same. You are grieving and I am sure I read somewhere that it's not just a straight line to get over someone when they die. More like a messy line of ups and downs, so I think this is totally normal to feel like this... you won't be sad forever."

"Maybe, but it doesn't feel exactly like that right now." He sighs again, staring at the floor.

"Is that why you are drinking, at school, on a school night?"

He smiles softly. "Amongst other things." He gazes at me as if he has only just realised the close proximity of our bodies and I see his eyes gaze down to my lips, but then quickly look back to my eyes. "You are so easy to be around, and to talk to. You just make me want to forget what responsibilities I have." He whispers that last part as if he doesn't want me to hear it, but I do. Okay, we are having a moment. I am pretty sure he has just declared he likes me. I am taking that as a win, for whatever game we are playing. I feel his gaze deepen, his warm whiskey breath on me. We are so close that if I just lean in, just a little, I could touch his lips with mine. Wanting the fantasy to become real makes me shudder with excitement.

"Is this the part where we kiss?" I whisper teasingly, as I slowly lean in towards him, I hear his breath catch, and I brush my lips against his.

"Absolutely not," he says. I pull back slightly, and he clears his throat, realising what was about to happen, he pulls away from the gaze and sits up.

Damn it, just kiss me already!

My heart breaks just a little bit more. "I'm sorry." He rubs his fingers on his temples and over his eyebrows. He is stressed. "I can't do this. This was a mistake."

I sigh in frustration.

"I don't get you, Zach! One minute you're hot, one minute you're cold. I can't win." He looks at me, his emotions tortured. "I get it, but why do you keep making us both unhappy, why do you keep resisting?"

"You are my student, I am your teacher, your dad is the head of this school, for crying out loud... If I lose control, if I let this be something else, and we get caught, I will lose my job, and I can't lose my job, I need this to su..." he stops talking suddenly, and I look at him.

"To what?" The silence is filled with our ragged breaths. He looks away, not wanting to continue the conversation. "What if I say you are worth the risk, we are worth the risk, that I want to be with you? Surely my feelings count in this. Surely, they matter?"

He lets out a frustrated moan.

"Of course, they matter. Do you know how hard this is for me?"

"Not really... you avoid me at all costs and share nothing." I want him to open up, he's so closed down and shut off. I want to stop caring because this is unbearable, but how do I do that? My heart, my body, even my soul wants him so much it's insane. No matter how brief, just a look, a touch, it's enough to spur me on this maddening flirty dance we have with one another. He sits down dejected and looks at me with that face from the first day back at school. "I am not good for you."

"Who says?" I scoot over in the chair back to his side and take his hand.

"You need to find someone your own age, someone who's more suited to your lifestyle and interests."

What the hell?

I snatch my hand back and stand from the chair, crossing my arms stubbornly.

"My own age, my own age! There's a 4-year difference between us, that's nothing, and my lifestyle, my interests, for crap sake Zach, you and I have the same lifestyle and interests, which, by the way, was very clear the first time we met."

He throws his hands in the air, he has no 'come back' but is not backing down. He opens the drawer, unscrews the whiskey bottle and pours himself another drink. He then flips open his book as if I am not there, again! Anger and frustration boil beneath the surface, and I take a few breaths before I say this sentence. I am hurt and angry. I feel so rejected and I have had enough. I can't keep doing this to myself, to my emotions.

"Fine, okay, that is fine, consider that the line is now drawn, no more of, whatever this is, I'm done! Do not cross it again, because I sure as hell won't. Goodnight Mr Jones."

Trying not to storm out like a brat, but making a quick exit, I slam the door and a quick sidestep to the toilet before my face explodes with yet another ugly cry, full of pumped-up rage and emotions. That man is damn right infuriating, and I am so sick of spending my time crying about him. I am officially done; I can't let my emotions and heart keep breaking like this.

I wish I didn't love him.

Twelve

I see you — Zach

I lean back into my chair with a frustrated groan. I watch her walk away, and her arse, wow, it's hypnotic. Man, I am an eejit, she is amazing. I want her so badly, and we almost kissed, *again!* But well-done brain, you resisted and remembered she is a student, so it is not allowed! I just know that the risk is too high, if anyone caught wind of this, my job, and my career would be over. Not to mention the safeguarding aspect, because she is still in my care, she is still in my class, and she is my student. It was another sick twist to my life story, but deep down in the corner of my mind, if I want to be honest with myself, I know she feels worth the risk. I know that much, but my head and heart were having this constant argument.

I can tell she has been avoiding me more too, which I am glad about, but it still hurts. Instead of blanking her in class, I have been feeling my eyes gravitating towards her, especially when she is composing, with her headphones on. She looks so deep in thought, her passion for music just emanates from her and it is so sexy. And that kind of passion has always been a turn-on for me. I see her side glances too.

I selfishly welcome them.

Some days I just want to grab her and kiss her like the first day we met, when I didn't know who she was and she didn't know who I was. That day was so simple. Perfect even. I have imagined every which way she tastes, moments of imagination where we are intimate, and the way she looks at me makes my dick ache. I know she wants me, and I want her so much. Her innocent look or near touch sends electric shocks of pleasure through my body. I have had to have a lot of alone time of late, just to get through the day. People may think I am a sick fuck having a wank in the toilet, but luckily, I share a toilet with only another male teacher and it's a locked, private cubicle. Sometimes if I don't blow my load, I would have to go home, because teaching her with a boner is not happening, *ever!*

I saw her in the library yesterday, her wavy, brown hair had fallen over some of her perfectly shaped face and a pencil was tucked behind her ear. She was so deep in concentration that she didn't see me staring. It made me smile at how beautifully perfect she looked. It had been so long since I liked someone, and I could not understand how life could be so fucked up in what we had created. I let myself stare for longer than I should, but I never am able to stare at her openly. Stolen glances, yes, all the time, but this, never this, and it was so well orchestrated as I needed a book that was in my line of sight.

So, I just take my time, and let it happen.

I let out a groan. Is this still a test? Because honestly, I feel I am due a break. I want her so bad and knowing it's forbidden, my messed-up brain wants her more. I sigh, looking away.

It's no good going down this road, let alone thinking about it, then STOP thinking about it, stop gurning!

In another life, maybe, but in this life, I need to be a realist and this realist has responsibilities. What a buck eejit. I sit at my desk for another hour, throwing the book to one side and decide to mark mock papers absentmindedly.

It's way after 10 pm now, so the band in the Music block will have finished practising and will have all gone home. I knock back the last of the drink and put it in my backpack. At least when I get home it will be quiet, I can happily finish this bottle whilst watching the match and I can just go to bed. Or maybe I won't and will just stay on the sofa!

Rock and roll, baby!

It didn't hit me until I step outside into the car park and walk over to my car that I had too much to drink, and I am not in any state to drive. Sure, I could risk the 5-mile or so drive home, but if I were caught it wouldn't be worth the hassle, the points, the money or even the jail sentence. I had to think rationally, again. Being a grown-up sometimes really is shit. I get into my car and sit there for a few minutes, contemplating walking or calling a taxi. I look up, and there she is.

Cora.

She is hard to ignore, walking across the car park. Thankfully she cannot see me and who is she with? Stefan. Dick. He seems to be saying something funny, as she is laughing. Although I can't hear it, I imagine how it sounds. In fact, I remember it, it's heart-warming. Her hair blows gently in the wind, and I think about how soft it would feel on my naked body. She is wearing that same flowery dress she wore on the first day of school, which curves both her breasts and her arse in such a good way. I sometimes struggle to even look at her in some of her outfits without thinking of all the things I wanted to do to her, often zoning out or excusing myself into the studio so that I could calm my racing thoughts and think of something revolting instead.

My heart stops for a moment as they both hug to say goodbye, and then Stefan kisses her. I feel so many emotions simultaneously, jealousy, anger, sadness – that was meant to be me – but the kiss is short-lived. She puts her hand on his chest. She looks very cross and steps away from him. It seems that this kiss was a surprise to both of us, and I can't help but smile that Stefan had been shot down by his advances. I realise my knuckles ache and my hands are white. I'm grabbing my steering wheel a wee bit too tightly.

"I have to let it go; I have to let her go," I whisper to myself.

Cora is standing on her own now. It seems that Stefan had made an embarrassingly quick exit, see ya, pal! Wow, that feels like the green-eyed jealousy monster has reared its ugly head. I close my eyes for a moment and rest my head on the steering wheel.

Get a bloody grip, Zachary, she is not yours.

When I open them, I realise that she's standing next to my car. Of course, of all the spaces in the school car park, she parked next to mine. She can see me now; I was hoping that in the sporadic car park lighting, she might have missed me. She hesitates as I look at her, then she opens the passenger door and bends her head down to look in the car, giving me a full cleavage view of her perfect breasts.

"Zach, are you okay?"

I can't help but wince when she says that because I love it when she says my name. It's music to my ears. I want to hear her moan my name when I kiss her lips and I want her to moan it again when I am buried deep inside her.

Ah, what an eejit. Stop doing this to yourself.

I lift my phone. "I am going to call a taxi, I thought everyone had left, I am a wee bit banjaxed." She looks confused. "Erm, drunk too much so I canny drive... so." She nods, hesitates, then sits in the car and shuts the door. "Erm... what are you doing?"

She sits there for a moment. "I'll drive you."

"What? No! A taxi is fine."

"For goodness sake, just let me give you a ride home, okay? You are drunk, I am not. I can drive you in my car, you cannot drive. Come on."

She doesn't look at me or wait for an answer as she gets out of the car. I guess I deserve that. I have told her to sod off, but here she is looking after me. She closes the door, opens my door and offers her hand. Man, she is even sexier when she's persistent and bossy. I take her hand. It is warm, soft, and she is beautiful.

The urge to cover my mouth over hers and slide my tongue into her sweet, wee mouth is growing, again. She leads me like a lost schoolboy to her car next to mine. A small Micra, very her style. She opens the door for me and semi-plonks me in there. I don't resist. I am quite enjoying being told what to do. Her car smells like tropical flowers, exactly like her, although I am unsure that it is wise telling her that she smells like her car. Not exactly a romantic compliment.

As we drive back to mine, I stare out the window, trying to avoid eye contact or saying anything to her at all. I am worried that if I do that, I will lose control. I shouldn't be alone with her. I cannot be alone with her. All of it goes to shit when we are alone.

But she doesn't make conversation. She switches on some music, a bit of old-school *Linkin Park*, which is surprising as she doesn't seem to me like the rock chick. Still, I didn't want to tell her that they are also one of my favourite bands too, as from the earlier conversation, it seems to me that the line had been drawn and she was done with whatever this was. I am nowhere near done. I like how she keeps on surprising me. She lightly sings along and nods her head to the beat. Her voice is so soothing, so soulful. I sigh, looking out the window, seeing the town so still, quiet and covered in darkness. It's different. Then we pass the ice cream shop that my mum used to take me to when we did our yearly visits to see my aunt. The sadness pangs again in my heart and takes me back to a particular time that leaves a bittersweet taste in my mouth.

It's been two years since my mum died and I am still fucking up any relationship that might be good for me. Maybe I don't deserve it. Maybe I don't deserve her. A few minutes later, I point to my house, and she pulls up onto the small drive.

"Nice house," she remarks.

I nod. It serves its purpose, a two up–two down. It's small but homely and I like it. Not far from school and the neighbourhood is friendly.

"Insurance pay-out from my mum." She nods again.

Okay, this is turning awkward and sombre. To my surprise, she turns the engine off and we sit quietly. It's nice to be in her company again, comfortable. She angles herself towards me and I can see she is conflicted about talking to me. She has that sweet wee crease in her forehead again and bites her lip.

She's nervous.

I lick my lips in anticipation. She is sexy when she is like this.

"Look, I am pretty sure you saw what happened back at school with me and Stefan and...."

My stomach drops, and the red light starts going off in my head again with that need to make her mine. Stefan, that piece of crap. Then the urge to kiss her is too hard to resist. After the evening I have had, and the drink, I have no fight left in me.

I want her.

I lean over and kiss her, and I remember how amazing she tastes, her soft lips on mine, the slight taste of cherry and her tongue perfectly fitting into my mouth. The way she smells, the small groans that escape her lips, to have that wrap around me, heaven.

She seems a wee taken aback at first but then eases into my kiss quickly. I deepen it, wanting to feel her closer, wanting to touch her so badly. She makes me feel consumed and from her heavy breathing, she feels the same. I lose myself in her as she loses herself in me. I went straight in for the touch. I need to have her. I trail my hand down her face, lightly over her collarbone and down into her bra. She shudders with excitement as I lightly tease her breasts. It feels so good to touch her, finally, after all those weeks of holding on, and it feels euphoric to let it all go. Even though my mind is exploding, telling me to stop, telling me this is wrong, I push that voice away. I push it as far away as possible because I no longer want to listen to the voice of reason. I don't want to give a shit about the consequences. She is eager to kiss back, and I want to lift her up and put her on my lap, stupid gearstick in the way. I trace my thumb over her nipple and feel it harden. Her breath is heavy and she is such a turn-on. I nibble behind her ear, leaving a trail of soft kisses down her neck. I feel her heart beating wildly. I move back to her lips and kiss her with more urgency and we move together in sync. I tease her mouth with my tongue and she teases my mouth with hers.

Her kisses are dangerous and addictive. I want all of her.

"Zach…" she whispers in a breathless tone. "Zach…stop…" I stop immediately, pull back and look into her eyes, which are full of desire. We both want this so badly. She looks away from me for a moment. "You don't want this… remember?"

I hang my head in shame. I do want this, I want this so bad. How can I tell her that? I cannot tell her that.

"I don't think I can do this." Hang on, isn't that what I am supposed to say? "I want you… so much, but you throw this wall up and I never know where I stand with you… you are driving me insane. I need to stay focused… I have my exams in less than eight weeks and I can't have every thought consumed by you. I just can't. I have worked too hard to mess up my exams." I hold her hand for a moment, contemplating her wise words, the disappointment in her voice is obvious. I feel it too. I lean my forehead against hers, and listen to her steady breath for a moment, closing my eyes just to remember this, because this had to be the end. She's right, I cannot keep doing this to myself. I cannot keep doing this to her. I cannot be half in or half out, or anywhere near her at all. I blow air out my mouth. This situation is fucked.

"I'm sorry."

I seem to say that to her a lot. She strokes my cheek lightly and I move back from her slowly. I look into her eyes, which seem almost black in the shadows of the night, or is that lust? Her cheeks are flushed and she looks so irresistible.

She pulls me back close and kisses me on the lips. I'm confused by what she said a moment ago – now we are kissing again. The desire kicks in even further. I am glad we are in the car, as the urge to rip off all her clothes and take her in the back seat of the car is strong but not one I want to tick off my bucket list. Plus, she deserves better than a backseat jump.

But why people do it, I understand now, the desire to have her close is crippling. I stroke my tongue over hers and another moan escapes. I love how she responds to me, but I am very pleased I wore my tight boxers today because otherwise, when I leave this car, it'd be rather embarrassing. I don't want this feeling to end, she turns me on. I feel all of her behind that kiss. But eventually, she pulls back and I stare at her again a wee bit confused.

"I just wanted one for the road. Now get out of my car, as I am not sure I can stop myself." I laugh at her; her grin shines brightly in the moonlight and for a moment everything just feels right. I get out of the car and watch her reverse out of my drive. She winds down the window where she meets my eyes with a smirk on her face. "See you, Mr Jones, now don't go falling in love with me, you should stay away from me altogether." And off she drove into the night, flipping her finger up at me, that was a low punch, but I deserved it.

Eejit.

Thirteen

Is blood thicker than water? —Cora

D o you ever get those days where you want to punch a stranger in the face? Because today I am definitely having one of those days. With trying to stay away from Zach and Stefan, I feel like my emotions are on the edge today and I am hating on life. Next-door-but-one thinks he is hilarious. When walking back from school today the old man decided to pipe up from his gardening work and say, "Cheer up, love, it might never happen." What is that saying even about?

1 – You do not know me; I could have had my whole family murdered and it actually DID happen – okay that was a little dark.

2 – Shut the hell up you're not funny.

3 – Also, do not talk to me, stranger danger.

4 – Now I want to resort to violence due to teenage rage and hormones and want to punch you in the face, Mr 'Perfect' front garden.

So, I do what any normal person would do and smile back and now he thinks he is the funniest person on the street. This just in from *Gardening World News*,

YOU ARE NOT FUNNY!

Dad could see the foul mood I was sporting when I arrive home, and because he is amazing, he doesn't question it. Instead, he ambushes Daisy and I for a family night out for dinner, saying that bonding and keeping the lines of communication open with his daughters were important to him. Because we had been working really hard at school and he's treating us to a nice dinner at the curry house in the town across from ours. Who am I to argue with that? Food makes me feel better. Good food makes me happier.

On the car ride over, Daisy is awfully quiet for her, in fact, she's been quiet all week, and she calls *me* a weirdo. I stare at her and her whole outfit is different, gone are the short skirts and crop tops, replaced with leggings and baggy jumpers, and her hair is not curled to perfection like her usual style, but scraped back into a sharp ponytail. And the make-up, or lack of it, is neutral, not the garish over-the-top blues or pinks, odd. She looks tired and I am half tempted to ask if she is okay, but then that would mean I care, or she'll bite my head off like usual, so I don't.

Dad is his usual cheerful self; talking about a scary film he went to see last night, not my cup of tea, but you like what you like. It seems he is very settled back at school and is happy in his secondment as a temporary headteacher, which I guess makes me happy too.

I thought having him as my dad and the headteacher at school would be odd, but it's not. I hardly see him, and we have different surnames, so it would seem no one has yet connected the dots. He was my headteacher at my school in Dubai, so any lasting weirdness evaporated ages ago.

We park up in a space 'round the back and head into the cosy restaurant. The delicious smells waft across the warm, well-lit room and make my tummy rumble as soon as I walk in the door. I am also glad it's not sub-zero temperatures like it has been the last few days, making me walk around in a cold shivering mess and wrapped up with so many layers, like the marshmallow man, it's suffocating. We seat ourselves in a corner booth at the back and Dad sits between us, which suits me fine. The waiter quickly takes our order, which I am pleased about because I am borderline hangry now.

"How is the application form for university going?" Dad asks as we tuck into our curries. I have ordered the classic chicken korma with a Peshwari naan. Dad orders a lamb something or other and Daisy has some vegetarian dish.

"Good, I have finished off my statement and I just need Za... Mr Jones to fill in my recommendation." Jeez, his name just slips off the tongue, no one seems to notice and if they did, they don't let on. Dad just nods and Daisy is lost in her phone.

"Deadline is next week, so I have plenty of time."

"Yes, but the earlier the better, then you know it is done." I agree, and Daisy excuses herself to use the toilet. We eat in silence for a few minutes and then I feel the back of my neck prickle. I look up to the takeaway counter and who's there, but Zach. The man I do not want to see, the man I am trying to avoid, yet here he is, in all his godliness, still in his suit from school and I am gawking and salivating like a starving person smelling food for the first time in days! Dad follows my eye line to Zach and laughs.

"Well, Zach, funny seeing you here, I can see you have good taste in food," my dad calls, and Zach turns to see who it is. I see his beautiful face mix with horror and awkwardness of this encounter. He grabs his takeaway bag from the counter and strolls over to the table with ease, all smiles and sporting some sexy stubble. That man recovers quickly. My dad stands and they shake hands.

"Well, it's the best curry house in the borough, Edward, good to see you," he politely nods at me and I remind myself to close my mouth. "Cora."

"Mr Jones," I splutter out, forcing a small smile.

"We were just talking about you," Zach looks a little confused. "Cora here is just finishing off her application for The Royal College of Music in London, she wants to use you as a recommendation."

"For sure," he replies without missing a beat, beaming down at me with his wide and flawless smile and I almost wet my knickers. "Cora is a very talented student, I am sure she will absolutely shine there."

Dad looks at me proudly and I don't know what to make of this situation. My dad and the man I'm secretly infatuated with (and stuck my tongue down the throat of only last week and then told him to stay away from me) in the same room. For once, I am speechless, so I just smile and shovel food in my mouth, so I don't have to speak. "It's a shame you were not at school before Christmas," Zach adds, "I take a day trip with the sixth formers to visit that university."

Dad's phone rings, he grabs it from his jacket pocket and looks at the caller with surprise.

"I have to take this, please excuse me." He disappears quickly from the table and exits the curry house. So, if it wasn't awkward a moment ago, it totally is now as we gaze at one another, not breaking eye contact, his face serious, devoid of emotion.

"London seems like a good shout, is that your first choice?" I nod, forcing a smile, unsure of what to say, he senses my unease. "About the other night, I feel like I should apologise, I was drunk and..."

"Don't do that," I murmur.

"Do what?"

"Apologise, like it was wrong, or that you regret it."

He leans down slightly and whispers, "It was wrong... but I don't regret it." His soft voice makes me shudder with excitement. He stands and straightens himself, our eyes meet, staying silent, I am coming undone, this man is all my fantasies rolled into one.

"What are you doing here?" Daisy comments as she walks back from the toilet. We break contact and he looks at Daisy and holds up his takeaway bag.

"Collecting dinner," he responds, and then Dad returns.

"Sorry about that, girls, important call. You still here Zach? You are welcome to join us."

"Oh, thanks, erm, no, I have company tonight, so I best be going anyway, nice to see you all." Then he strides away with his long, manly legs. I try not to look at him for too long as he leaves, as I can feel Daisy staring at me.

I feel sick. Company? What company?

Fourteen

Stefan is a douche —Cora

The following week, I threw myself into my studies. However, my thoughts always returned to Zach, it was infuriating, and I could not think of much else. But the decision to go cold turkey felt like a good idea, even though it was killing me. Did he want to be with me? Did I want to be with him? We went back to our normal routine of ignoring one another. I would often see him on duty during lunch or break, but he seemed preoccupied and didn't seem to seek me out.

Nevertheless, music is still my favourite lesson to stare at this man-god. But an interesting development, this week, I even caught him (a few times) staring back and, mixed in with that sexy kiss a few weeks back, has given me a new confidence boost to obsess over him even more. During lessons, when he calls upon the class with questions about music or the upcoming A-level exams, I try to give heartfelt and meaningful answers, and for those short moments, it feels like we are connected again and he is staring into my soul. I have left class several times turned on by his brooding look, and it's slightly embarrassing how just one look would turn my whole body on fire.

My sister seems to always pop into my music lesson before, after, and even sometimes during, coming up with the excuse that she had come on her period, again, and needed a tampon. Pretending to let her eyes roam around the room. But I knew the reason why, she wanted to 'goo-eye' at

Zach and it was really annoying. I felt like I needed to cat wee all over him to state my territory, that he was mine, even though I knew he wasn't, but you get my point. I even came up with a fun fantasy that when all this was over, we could be together. Even though my head was telling me I was full of shite, my heart was on a whole new fantasy level and there were days where I rocked between my heart and my head, just to survive his lesson; his look, his face, it was torture.

Music lessons were always bittersweet.

I would be so excited to see him and yet I did not want to see him. I was torn with how I felt about him and all the toing and froing in my mind was emotionally draining. Despite this, I am happy that I have been more focused on my studies and working towards my examination. And I am almost ready to submit my application to the university in London. It is under a two-hour drive from home and it satisfied Dad's overprotective stance of, 'don't go too far away from home.'

But today I need to see Zach. I needed to go and get my recommendation for my application to the university. I feel weak at the knees just thinking about him, alone in the room. My head and my heart want to see him today, so this is a great excuse. I casually walk into his room at lunch, hoping he would be there, and stop still in the doorway – what I did not expect is another lady teacher with him. Miss Miller. Sitting at the table chatting, laughing, eating lunch together, like a fucking date.

Is this the company he had last week when we saw each other at the curry house?

Her dress is short, her legs are long, and her pretty red hair is tied up in a ponytail, and they were laughing, *laughing*. Let's be honest, nothing is that funny, and my face turns into a scowl.

'Don't frown Cora or the lines will be there for life.' Why does Mum always pop into my head like this?

Pushing that aside, it then hits me dead in the chest. I am jealous. Here is a lady, who's around his age. She is someone he can date openly, not someone he needs to hide or keep secret. Someone he can take to dinner, someone he can walk hand in hand in public to the cinema, take home and be proud of. Not a dirty little secret, not someone like me. I turn to walk away as I feel the hot tears rising and prickle my eyes, threatening to spill over. Cursing myself as this is ridiculous because this thing, we had is over. Something I want so badly it hurts, and I feel like this whole situation is so unfair. This relationship we had sucks and another piece of my heart is broken.

"Cora?" Zach squeaked. I turn back, swiping my face discreetly, hoping another tear wouldn't spill over.

"Everything okay?" Miss Miller looks really peeved I have interrupted their lunch date. Good, bitch. I clear my throat, hoping my voice comes out steady.

"I can see you're busy, sir, sorry. I just wanted to see if you could write my letter of recommendation for university?"

"Of course, not a problem," he looks down at Miss Miller. "I am a bit busy this lunchtime. Can you come back after period 5 and I can have a look?" The smug look on Miss Miller's face makes the *Gardening World* old man seem like nothing.

I want to drown her!

I plaster the fakest smile that I can summon from the bottom of my soul, feeling like I am pushed aside, again.

"Yes, of course, sir, thanks very much."

With that, I retreat, like a skittish ostrich high tailing it out of there, and thanking my deep, inner eyelids that I did not just go in and cry, like a crazy person. He is not mine; he will never be mine and I need to accept this.

Six weeks left, Cora, six weeks.

I do not want to cry over this anymore.

I return after period 5, mentally prepping in my head to ask about bitch face Miss Miller but basking in the thought that we will be alone, again, and I feel oddly excited. However, I have a feeling in the pit of my stomach, knowing it is not a good idea to be alone in his company because that is when my obsession gets worse and I need to stay focused. I have been doing so well! Before chickening out, I detour to the girl's toilet. I reapply my lip gloss, run my fingers through my wavy hair, readjust the girls and head to the Music block. But it seems it was all in vain, there are a few other pupils there who are also having their recommendation letters signed.

He really does not want to be alone with me.

Deflated, I sit and wait for my turn and after several minutes, they are all done, filtering out one by one.

"Cora, I'll do you next." I wish. I watch as he fills in the form with all the details from school and his tick-box answers. The last person leaves and we both become acutely aware that we are alone. His leg starts bouncing as if he is nervous. I put my hand on his knee to stop. I don't want him to be nervous. I just want him. He stops writing and looks at me, those eyes, those lips, I can't get enough of him. His jaw clenches. I can see him fighting with himself, with his morals and the desire, that pulls between us. He sighs and gently moves my hand away and continues to finish my recommendation.

"There we go. I will email the recommendation and some of your music samples directly over to the university this week."

He smiles and pushes the paper over so that I can sign it. I deliberately touch his hand as I give it back to him. He frowns, pulling his hand away quickly, and folding his arms over his chest. "Now if you'll excuse me, I am quite busy." He practically storms out of the room.

Rude.

I drive home shortly after, glad that it is the end of the day and happy I don't have to drive Daisy home or go anywhere else. I just want to get into my PJs and wallow in self-pity. Apparently, Dad purchasing this car is great for me, but it has also made me a personal taxi service to my sister. And when moaning to Dad about it, he practically threw me under the bus, saying that it was definitely one of the reasons why he purchased it for me in the first place. When I walk into the house, I can smell the garlic and butter, it makes me groan hungrily. Dad is home early today, which I thought was odd and when I enter the kitchen, I can see he has already started dinner. It is the classic family lasagne, one of my firm favourite dinners.

"Smells nice,"

"Thanks, lovely. How was school?"

"Good. I have my university application and it is all ready to be emailed over." He looks at me with pride.

"Good girl, so what are you waiting for?" I look at him, confused. "Go send it. Dinner won't be for another hour." He's looking tired around the eyes.

"I will. I want to read through it one last time. Hey, Dad?"

"Hm?"

"You okay?"

"Yeah, I just left work early, as I had a migraine. Nothing like a good dinner to sort that out. I think the last few months are catching up on your old Dad." He smiles, but it doesn't quite reach his eyes.

The next morning, after yet another shitty sleep, I am going for a can-do attitude – today is a new day. After posting my application, I made a very adult decision about Zach. Even though I don't appreciate his cold attitude towards me, I will respect it. If that's how he deals with keeping away from me, that's fine. We have to stay away from one another. I know nothing good will come out of this if I keep trying to push him or myself and I finally feel okay with that. And to demonstrate that feeling, I am wearing my lucky socks and walk into school with an extra smile.

But as I arrive at school, something is seriously wrong. Everyone is looking at me oddly, like I have something written on my face. People are whispering and laughing, and I don't know what it is and I am definitely not imagining it. I run to the girl's toilet and look into the mirror, thinking it is something on my face or my hair. But nothing. Then a text comes through from Sophie.

Girl, where are you? There are some shit rumours flying around school about you.

I almost stop breathing, it feels like my world is collapsing down on me and I can't breathe. I must have been found out; they know. I instantly throw up and empty my stomach. I just couldn't understand how, we had been discreet, well at least I thought we had. My dad will kill me, and Zach will lose his job. This is just not what was meant to happen. I text Sophie back, letting her know where I am. When she arrives a few minutes later, I am sitting on the dirty floor of the girl's bathroom with my head in my hands, trying to breathe through a really nasty anxiety attack. Sophie comes in and kneels by my side and strokes my hair like an awesome friend. We sit there for a few minutes until I get my breathing under control.

"It's okay Cee Cee, it's okay."

"How did people find out?" My breathing now returned; the sobbing starts.

"Stefan and his big mouth, he can't keep it shut."

"Stefan?" I raise my head with bleary eyes.

"He's a twat bag, Cee Cee..." Sophie grabs some tissue and hands me some. I wipe my eyes and nose. "So, it's true then?"

I nod, I might as well come out with it, no point in the lie now. She whistles. "Well, it's done now, I mean, everyone's talking about it. People just love to gossip." Some Year 9 girls walked in and stare at me like I am possessed, I swear one of them is about to take a picture of me. "Piss off!" shouts Sophie and they retreat sheepishly. I love Sophie, she is a strong, confident woman, the woman I want to be. "Look, don't cry over him. He's a douchebag if he says things like that." I look up, confused. "At least you lost your V card, you know, silver linings," she continues.

Wait, what? I stop crying completely.

"What are you talking about?" I look up at her as she's sitting on the toilet, stall open and having a wee.

"You know, you and Stefan?"

"Me and Stefan what?"

"Shagging, sexing, doing the deed, saying hooray, no more V card."

"I definitely did not have sex with Stefan." She wipes herself and flushes the toilet, redoing her skirt back to a very short level. She washes her hands and then looks at me.

"I don't get it. So, you are saying you didn't lose your V card to Stefan?"

"No... what has he been saying?" The utter sadness a few moments ago, is now changing into simmering anger.

"Okay, I am just going to say what I heard as there's no point sugar-coating this crap..." she sighs and continues, "he said that you had sex with him, he said it was shit, your vag stinks and he couldn't continue so you gave him a blowy and he had to stop 'cause that was worse... oh, and you can't kiss." I sit there, stunned into silence, which I have to say was another first for me. "Wait, if you didn't shag him, what are you talking about? Why are you in here crying?"

Shite, this was bad.

"Nothing. I thought you were talking about something else." She eyes me suspiciously as I change the subject. I will deal with that later if I have to. "What an absolute cock, why... why would he say that?" She shrugs. "Everyone knows?"

"Of course everyone knows. He probably said it because you didn't put it out."

My stomach drops again, of course, it's about that, but what if Zach hears about this, or Dad?

Shite, this is a different kind of bad. I stand up and wipe my face again. I am not having this. The whole school thinks I slept with that arse and then he said I stink.

That is a school nightmare. I hate confrontation, and I hate Stefan, but to hell, if he thinks I will keep quiet.

I storm out of the toilet. "Where is he?" It doesn't take long to find him, he's where he usually is, in the dining hall. Luckily, most people haven't filed in for breakfast before the first period yet, so it was pretty empty. I can hear Sophie trying to call me back and telling me to leave it, but I just block her out. This isn't her fight; she can't save me and for once, I need to fight my own battles. He sees me coming and I know I look a mess, but fuck this. No one should ever have fake rumours thrown around school about them.

Deep breaths, Cora.

He carries on talking to his friends, not even acknowledging me. I am not standing up for just myself. I am standing up for all the girls and boys that have had rumours spread about them, just for liking or sleeping with someone and then being called a slag for it, why do people do that? It's so messed up.

"Why would you say that, Stefan?" He looks at me whilst sitting on the table, feet on the chair, like he's on his throne, thinking he's some cool person. But I can see who he is. A sadistic piece of shit, who couldn't take no for an answer, probably because no one had ever said no to him before.

"Say what exactly? What's wrong with your face Cora? You look a mess!" Some of his friends' snicker. "In fact, you look mental." Of course, he would say that, that's what people used to call my mum, 'mental.'

"I've been crying, you idiot."

"Not my problem." He turns his back to me. I put my hand on his shoulder with force and move him back around.

"It *is* your problem if you think it's okay going around saying to people that we slept together – when I wouldn't touch you with a 10-foot pole."

"Well, we didn't quite sleep together, you know, because of, you know…" he leans in closer, "your personal hygiene problem." My eyes almost bulge out of my head. He and his friends burst out laughing and I just see red!

"Come on, Cora, just leave this sad sack of shit," Sophie whispers trying to pull my arm away gently. I unhook it and glare back at Stefan.

"Fuck you, you couldn't even get it up if you tried, your penis is so small that I wouldn't even be able to find it." I fire back. A few of his friends start oooooooooing at the situation, which Stefan does not like.

He slinks off the table and stands up right next to me, in my face, all smiles gone now, as if that would intimidate me. I am not afraid of him, and I've had a lot of standoffs with Daisy, and she is definitely scary when she gets going. This is personal and I can feel my body shaking with anger.

"Well, you did try your best," he responds sarcastically. "But I couldn't go through with it, it was so bad. I mean your face is pretty and all but underneath Cora, underneath, it's a disaster. Like a smelly, car crash disaster. I thought things were bad with ya mum, but you know, it seems things run in the family." I feel like I'm going to die. His words are hurtful and degrading, no girl wants to hear shite talk about herself in public, it's mortifying. True or not, no one had the right to talk about me like this, behind my back or to my face and bringing my mum into this is an all-time low. I just can't do it anymore.

All that rage comes flooding back, my mum, the heavy drinking and then her arrest. All the whispers, all that crap my family tried to get away from by leaving here. Now Stefan has dragged it all up again and all because I said no and hurt his ego. Stefan thinks that humiliating me in public will help fill his ego, that I will let him say these things to me and it's okay. I won't have this. And then something snapped.

"What the fuck, Stefan!" Sophie spits out. But I am so engulfed in fury that I barely register her words.

I ball my fists up and, as hard and fast as I can, I hit him in the cheek. The noise from it is not the sound I'm expecting, like a crack and a slap at the same time. I put all my rage for him, Zach, mum and all the shit surrounding my life and throw it into that punch. Everyone is eerily silent. My hand hurts so bad, but I will not show my pain.

"Did you just hit me? You fucking crazy bitch-"

"Cora! Stefan!" I cringe and turn. I know that voice. I let out an inward sigh. My stomach drops. Of all the people I don't want to hear this, it's Zach. Yet here he is, in the middle of the hall, standing with a bowl of cereal in hand, oh yeah, teachers come in and get breakfast here too, great. "My room, now!" he bellows.

Stefan's group of friends start to laugh and then disperse, saving their own arses so they don't get into trouble. I look to Sophie; she throws me a pitiful glance and walks out as she also knows waiting around will get her detention too. I follow Zach and Stefan to the Music block, head hanging down and my thoughts going a mile a minute.

Once there, he slams the door closed and barks at us to sit. I flinch when he does but am slightly surprised that I am a little turned on by his anger. That's definitely something I might want to explore. Zach walks over to the side fridge, removes a cold compress from it and throws it gently to Stefan. He catches it easily and puts it on his very red cheek. I inwardly smile.

Dick.

Stefan's eyes are still full of rage. Probably because he has been hit by a girl and now his school social credit has gone down the pan. Or maybe he finally got the fricking hint that I don't want to be with him. Zach sits on the edge of the desk.

"Mind telling me what's going on?" I keep my eyes down, staring at his shiny brown shoes and his rather large feet. This is one of the shittiest and most embarrassing moments of my life. I can't look him in the eye about this. I can barely breathe. What must he think of me now? "…Cora…" I shake my head slowly, keeping my eyes cast down, "…Stefan…" He just stares ahead. Now he shuts his mouth. "Shall I tell you what I saw? I saw and heard a heated argument and I saw you, Cora, hit Stefan… I am sure you are very well aware that is against school rules and is a punishable action if not detention and/or an internal exclusion at least… your parents will be notified…" I let out a sigh and I hear Stefan do the same. Zach heard what Stefan said to me. I feel so hurt, and embarrassed.

I feel like a fool.

Zach sits back around at his desk and continues to eat his breakfast. I feel his cool stare on us both, waiting us out. I don't even know what to say. I feel bad that I hit him. I have never resorted to violence in my life, felt it and thought about it many times, but I never acted on it. But jeez, it felt good.

He deserved it.

I was standing up for myself and for womankind, who never get the chance to face their demons or the dickheads who lie, cheat or create blasphemy about their vagina, and gave it back, full force. No one talks about my girl like that and she doesn't stink. I keep her very well-maintained. But he wouldn't know that because he has never seen it or been anywhere near it, the little shite. I steal a look at Zach who is boring his eyes into me. What do I say? What can I say?

Although his eyes are saying it all: disappointment, disgust. My stomach is in knots and a wave of sadness engulfs my body. No one should be looked at like this. Another piece of my heart shatters. I must look like a bloody catty child, my hair all over the place, my eyes rimmed red from crying, but I was angry, and I can express my emotions the way I damn well like. "Are we just going to sit here all morning? Someone needs to tell me what is going on."

"Cora is fucking mental, that is what is going on." I glare at him; I hope his whole face bruises.

My hand was starting to ache more, but I would wear this pain like a badge of honour and right now I would happily hit him again – maybe with the other fist.

"Language Stefan, do not swear and I do not appreciate that sentence either, saying someone is mental."

"Well, she is, we slept together and she doesn't like the fact that everyone knows." I cringe at his words and feel all the air being sucked out of the room. Zach chokes on his cereal for a moment and carefully put the bowl on the table. I look at Zach, sad and hurt cross his eyes briefly, but then it's gone and he continues without missing a beat. Zach is a damn professional in keeping his face neutral and pan-faced.

"Right, well," he clears his throat. "I am sure that any young woman would like to keep her personal details private and obviously, I am here to also preach about safe sex as well." I wanted the ground to swallow me up and die. A death by one of those creatures from Stranger Things would be kinder than this moment right now. This is worse than the sex talk I got from Dad in Year 9!

Just breathe, Cora.

It's all BS and we know that the way I act now is the reflection that I want Zach to see, a mature, less violent woman.

I can do this.

Zach looks expectantly at me, begging me to say something. I sit tall and turn to face Stefan.

"I apologise for hitting you." He smiles at me as if he has won the battle, but just you wait, you turd face. I turn to Zach because shit is about to get real. I stare straight into his eyes so he could see I was telling the truth. He must know that I am not this person, sleeping around, swearing, fighting, he must think so little of me now.

"But I don't regret it. Sir, Mr Jones, I would like to explain the reason why I hit him. I want to 100% clear up the fact that we did NOT sleep together, nor on any level would I want to engage with or be near someone like him. The thing is, Stefan decided to pressure me into things I did not want to do, he kissed me, and I asked him not to. He told me I should give him a blowjob, I said no, and then he said we should sleep together, I said no, again. So even though I told him on many occasions that I did not want to involve myself in any of that, his harassment of sex towards me has been unbearable. It's clear that I have said no on many occasions and yet he does not seem to get the answer, respect me, or respect my boundaries. Yet because of my continual rejection, I think I wounded his pride, or ego, or whatever. So he has then decided to spread rumours about us sleeping together and some very nasty ones at that." Stefan started to cough over his laughter.

"You stink," Stefan mutters and I glare at him.

D.I.C.K. H.E.A.D.

"Is this true?" Zach asks ignoring the comment. Stefan just looks through him not denying or agreeing. "Because if it is, Stefan, this is a serious allegation."

"Yes, we kissed, a lot and she loved it, but all the rest is crap, sir. Can't you see she's making it up? She's mental, she won't leave me alone."

Students start to file into the Music room. Period 1 is about to start. Zach lets out a big sigh.

"I need to teach a class now. You are both in detention after school. I expect to see you both here at 3:15 pm and to write an account of what has actually happened and I will speak to both of your parents about this. And as for the consequence, we will decide on how to proceed with this further after school, *tonight*. Do you understand?" We both nod and leave.

I try to lie low for the rest of the morning, but the whole school knew and the staring and the laughing increased. Some looked on in pity but mainly, it was laughing. The entire morning made me continually think about Mum, her arrest, the pain and heartache that caused. Even though I had thicker skin now and could drown out most of the crap, it still hurt like a bitch. So, I opted to hide in the toilet between breaks, which seemed like the best plan.

Until after lunch, when I was pulled out of English by Dad. Another great horror and embarrassment. He had also heard the rumours (what is wrong with this school) and was furious. He was red in the face and tried not to shout but I could see he was hurt and disappointed. Even when I tried to tell him the whole story, he said he understood, but he never said he believed me, which made me feel like a bad daughter.

I hate disappointing him.

If he is so angry over this, he will literally flip his lid if he found out the real story between me and Zach. Just after the last period, I walk towards the Music room and Stefan's group of friends start to sing, 'There She Blows', instead of, *'There She Goes'* by *The La's* song. I roll my eyes so hard I think I see the back of my head. This is ridiculous, and where is Sophie when I need her? I haven't seen her since this morning and have texted her a bunch of times and she hasn't even read them.

Today, I feel really alone.

I roll up to the Music room at 3:15, ready to take my punishment but looking a lot more presentable, and surprise, surprise, Stefan doesn't turn up, which to be honest, is a relief. I hope I never see him again. I recount everything, in detail, on paper and then painfully watch Zach read it.

He doesn't say anything or look at me. He puts it in an envelope and places it in his desk drawer and then continues to mark books. I work quietly on some coursework to pass the hour. Zach barely looks at or speaks to me, which hurts a little, but I can see that he is still simmering with anger. Miss Miller, the art teacher, seems to filter in and out a lot and casually flirts here and there, which adds fuel to my fire.

My heart hurts. I want this hour to end.

"Is it true… did you sleep together?" He asks, breaking the silence just before the hour is up. He sits behind his desk, deep in thought. The question hurts me. But I guess we really do not owe each other anything. The fact that he thinks that makes my heart sink, and I feel the last slither of my heart shatter. Is he asking because he cares or, is he asking because he needs to write this incident up? Or maybe he doesn't believe me, just like Dad.

"No," I whisper, "no, we didn't. Yes, we did kiss, but you know that already." We stare at each other for a few moments, his face unreadable and then he looks away.

"You may go. I haven't spoken to your Dad yet... but I will."

"Don't bother. He already knows." I leave the room, knowing this is the end. He is looking at me differently, as if I am a stranger. That I am someone he does not want to associate with anymore.

This is definitely over.

Fifteen

Don't leave me —Cora

A few weeks later, I am standing in Dad's office. It's his birthday tomorrow and I decide to wait around school until his Governor's meeting was over so we could go out and eat some sort of pub dinner, probably pie.

Daisy was running late as usual.

I hover with the door open, hoping to catch Zach, but to no avail. To be honest, I have tried to keep a low profile since that day with Stefan. We both received an internal exclusion and from then on Zach has been distant too. He's gone back to hardly looking at me, and even if I don't want to look at him, my heart does and my eyes wander. Maybe I am not the mature woman I thought he needed after all. Even though the situation wasn't my fault, I feel disappointed in myself.

I took a few days off last week because I had the dreaded flu, but I overplayed it to Dad because I didn't want to be in school. People still look at me, ignore me, or whisper things as I walk past.

But to be honest, it's just like before we left, when mum was convicted and sent to jail. I was the talk of the town, and no one let me forget it then and I was silly to think they would forget it now. But Easter break is almost upon us and then after that, there are less than 2 weeks left until exams, so this will be short-lived. After about half an hour, I flick through my phone and work through social media to cure my boredom.

Dad finally returns and throws an 'I am sorry you waited so long,' smile and starts to pack up his briefcase. But then he suddenly stops. I look over at him, he has gone as white as a sheet and his forehead looks clammy; he slumps back onto his chair.

"Dad? Are you okay?" He falls from the chair to the floor and I let out a scream. I run over to him, and he is sort of foaming a bit at the mouth with his eyes rolled back. Mrs Rowe, the school's personal assistant comes bustling in from all the commotion. "My dad, he's collapsed!" I scream at her.

She is on the phone immediately, whilst I stroke Dad's hair and I try to lay him in the recovery position. All those stupid mini-courses Dad sent me on finally come in handy. I push him carefully over onto his side, with his hand on his head and his knee up. I check he is still breathing, which thankfully he is, his heartbeat is slow, but it's still there.

I hold his hand tight, tears stinging my eyes.

A few people have gathered in the room now, and of course, Zach is here now. He is putting a blanket over Dad, so he isn't cold. This is that part in the film where time slows down, and all I can hear is my own ragged breathing and the pulsing sound of my erratic heart.

Is this also the part where he dies?

Panic sweeps through me and I look at Zach helplessly, he pulls me into a hug, which shocks me momentarily, PDA. But then I realise that this is a 'you need help and support' hug and no one bats an eyelid. They just look afraid for Dad and concerned for me. The ambulance arrives a few minutes later and the responders put an oxygen mask over his face. They cut open his shirt and put some sticky pads over his chest to monitor his heart. They say how everyone has done a great job, although I don't see how that is even possible as Dad is not really conscious. Mrs Rowe offers to ride in the ambulance with me but they say only one person. I thank her gratefully, tell her to bring Daisy to the hospital and trudge after the trolley, where Dad lies all strapped in and ready to go. I hear Zach say he will walk with me to the car park to the other staff and catches me up halfway down the corridor.

"Do you need anything?" I look at him through blurry eyes.

"No," is all I can muster up.

I walk silently to the ambulance and watch as they load Dad into the back on the stretcher. Zach takes my hand, but I can't bear to take my eyes off Dad.

"You have my number. Please ring or text if you need me." I nod and give him a fake 'I am okay don't worry' smile, but it's a miserable attempt because he looks at me with worry and sadness, so it didn't work.

This must be bad.

He holds me close again momentarily, I don't need this right now so I pull away and I climb into the back, sitting next to Dad and holding his hand. The doors close with one of the medical staff in the back and the lights are on and we are off, speeding through the streets to the hospital. It strikes me how the ambulance is so white and bright. I am surprised they don't wear sunglasses or something. The smell of bleach or cleaning products is so overwhelming, I nearly gag. I hear the driver radio into the hospital, possible heart attack I hear her say, although I am not really paying attention. It seems everything is whirling by, and I can't keep my eyes off Dad or my mind still. I then start to dry heave and the man offers a bag which I vomit into. He doesn't look concerned, but I guess he does this every day. This is his job. How many times can you see a person die before you become de-sensitised?

We arrive several minutes later; Dad is wheeled through to the A&E entrance around the side. I am told to go into reception, book him in and wait. After an hour of pacing the reception area of A&E, a text comes through from Zach.

Any news?

I ignore it. My phone goes again, this time it's Sophie.

Girl, just heard through the grapevine, you okay?

Ignore, ignore, ignore. I throw my phone in my bag and groan with frustration. Daisy looks up from her chair, rolling her eyes, looking like this is my fault. When she arrived, she was all sorts of angry, even though we hugged and we cried. What else can we do now but wait? Waiting is the worst. Another hour slips by and I honestly feel like I am going to kill someone. People are coming and going and I am still here. Still here, waiting, sitting on this pathetic piece of plastic crap the hospital calls a chair. My bum is numb. I want to start shouting profanities to get some attention and answers. Ding goes the phone. Zach again.

I am still awake if you need anything.

Ahhh, I want to send a one-fingered emoji through the phone. He can't text me back *ever* when I text him. I honestly thought he gave me the wrong number, but he's happy to send two texts in two hours.

The door swings open. "Wilkinson?"

"Me," I squeak.

The doctor gestures for us both to follow him and we eagerly do, wanting answers, wanting anyone to explain. We follow him to a cubicle where Dad lies topless, hooked up to every which machine. I put my hand over my mouth as I gasp, he looks dead.

"I know it can seem frightening, with all the monitors and machinery, but he is in good hands. We have stabilised him and from our test results and ECG scan, it seems your dad has had a heart aneurysm. Sort of like a mini-heart attack. Now, this was a warning sign from his body."

"Is he going to be okay... is he going to die?" Daisy whispers.

"Your Dad is lucky... we need to keep him in for a few days to monitor him, run some more tests and see if he needs any surgery. We also need to ensure we have the right medication and a plan going forward. Can I contact your mum or other family members?" I shake my head. Dad is always so calm and collected. He never seems stressed out or under pressure, well, not normally. He said he felt unwell the other week, maybe I should have taken better care of him or asked more questions to see how he was.

"Just us," I add. He nods in understanding and pity.

"I will give you some time alone, but don't stay too long. You both need to rest."

I sigh with relief, and sit next to Dad on the bed, holding his hand. With the consistent slow beep of the monitor and Dad's pale face, he looks like he's aged ten years in a day. How could this have happened – were there any warning signs I could have picked up on if I had been paying attention? I had been so caught up in Zach that even if there were any, I had failed to notice and it made me feel like a shitty daughter. That this was my fault somehow.

After a while, I decided to text both Sophie and Zach the same message.

Heart attack, keeping him in for a few days, am going home to sleep, and will talk to you tomorrow.

After calling a taxi, I switch my phone off and wait outside on a bench, what a nightmare. Daisy didn't want to leave his side and the nurse made up a side bed for her. The nurse said the sedation would keep him asleep until tomorrow and Daisy's hysterical crying was sending me over the edge. I know she's upset but watching her was as painful as sitting and watching Dad lie so still, with the constant beep, beep, beep.

I am barely holding on myself.

Visiting time was over and I was glad for the escape. I felt suffocated in there, the smell of hospitals fills me with dread. Not that I have had a bad experience there, I just feel everyone else's bad experiences flow through me and fill me with anxiety.

But I guess this was my time to have the unwanted experience of being there. I am happy the driver doesn't take long to turn up or want to talk. Even though it's only 11 pm, I lay my head back on the seat and close my eyes. I feel drained of energy, that my soul has been sucked out, played a good game of football and thrown back into my body. I arrive home and pay the driver. I walk up to the house and realise someone is parked on the drive. It quickly dawns on me that it is Zach's car.

My heart drops, well at least I know it is still working.

Sixteen

The first time — Cora

I do not see him at first, but as I walk closer to the front door, I see him sitting on the front garden bench, hidden in the shadows. His face looks relieved to see me and I wonder how long he has been waiting. He pulls me into a hug and feeling him close is a relief. Seeing a friendly face, and having to deal with all that, I didn't realise how lost I felt, and he just makes everything feel better.

That I am not alone.

Luckily, there's no pissed-off face from our last encounter, no looking at one another like strangers, just those caring, loveable brown eyes. I feel like I can breathe again.

"How are you doing?" He looks at me as the tears involuntary stream down my face.

"Better." I wipe them away with my sleeve.

"Let's get you inside."

I open the door and he lets himself in. It feels weird having him here, in my house. A mixed feeling, I can't begin to sort out, but oddly comforting. He takes off his rucksack and produces a bottle of red wine. "I thought you might need this." I smile gratefully and fall onto the sofa with a sigh.

He wanders to the kitchen and returns a few moments later with two large glasses. He pours the wine; I take it and down the whole glass. I need it and don't choke, for once. He arches his eyebrow at my action and then he offers his. I take it and he pours another glass for himself. We sit in silence, whilst nursing our drinks. He doesn't take his eyes off me. Even though any glance would usually excite me, I only feel broken and numb. After he finishes his glass, he moves closer to me on the sofa, takes my glass out of my hand, and guides me to rest my head on his lap. He pulls the blanket over my body and starts to stroke my hair and I close my eyes with a contented sigh enjoying his soft and soothing touch.

I awake maybe an hour or two later, I didn't mean to fall asleep, the exhaustion of the evening must have taken over. I sit up slowly and notice the TV is on, it is a re-run of *Friends* and I see that Zach is asleep. How can a man who passes out sat up on my sofa, mouth open, slightly snoring still look unbelievably beautiful? I watch his chest rise and fall, it's peaceful.

He is my one, despite this shitstorm.

He's my first love and I love him so much it hurts. I can't believe he is here, he came for me, he wanted to comfort me and be by my side. Surely that's a sign, a sign that he likes me and that he still wants me. I am sitting so close to him on the sofa that I start to feel that excitement building into a hum.

We are alone. There is no dad, no sister, no school, no prying students, no teachers, just me and him. I stare at him and trace my eyes all the way down his body, I want him so bad. I feel it deep in my core, a want so deep, I can't ignore it anymore, so why not?

I climb over to him, straddle myself on top of him, and kiss him softly on the lips. He wakes startled and then realising where he is, his body relaxes.

"You, okay?" he asks groggily, rubbing his eyes. I nod and kiss him softly again; he looks up at me. "What time is it?"

"A little after one," I murmur the words on his lips.

"Do you want me to go?" He asks awkwardly. I let out an exaggerated sigh, lean back from his perfect mouth and look at him. "I can go if you want me to... or I can stay?"

Obviously, the pouty face must have shown through which is music to my ears. Of course, I want him to stay, I definitely do not want to be alone right now, and he is in my house. We are alone, oh, my, freaking heck, we are in my house, alone. Panic and excitement consume my body, but then my brain kicks in a little.

"What is the real reason you came here tonight, Zach?"

He looks taken aback by the question. His eyes search mine. I can see he cares for me, but I want to hear him say it. I want him to admit it. I desperately wanted to hear him say it out loud. So many backwards and forwards over the last few months.

"Why do you think?" I sigh, he never gives me a straight answer and I am too tired for his games, I lean back a little more.

"I don't know what to think. What I want to hear is the truth, not what I think, or what other people should think or feel, or what the school might say, or stupid rumours from stupid boys, or my dad. I just want to hear what you have to say, what you feel, and think."

He lets out a defeated sigh and looks at me. Is this finally the moment of truth, where we can be really honest with one another?

"I shouldn't feel these things, for you, but I do. I tried so hard to be professional, to be the *good* guy. Being with you puts my job on the line, but I can't seem to stay away from you... I better go..."

My stomach drops at his decision to leave and now I am getting desperate. He goes to move me off, but I dig the heels of my feet into the sofa and put my hand on his chest.

"Just stop." I put a finger on his lips. "Stop talking. Do you hear that?"

He pauses for a moment. "No?" He looks towards the door in a panic as if we are going to be caught.

"Exactly, silence... no one is here... no one knows you are here... just shut up and kiss me."

He realises what I am saying and I gently kiss his lips again and this time he kisses me back. He touches my face and rubs his thumb along my cheek and jawline, and I melt into his touch, just as I did when we first met, and I shudder with excitement. He pulls away slightly, and his eyes search mine again. I want him, and from the dark hunger in his eyes, he wants me too, bad.

I let out a shaky breath.

He leans slowly in towards me, and I feel his tender lips on mine. I feel safe and wanted and that is exactly what I need right now. I need this. I need him, I need to feel something, I need to forget, and he seems to know that to be soft, to be gentle. I deepen the kiss and he groans into my mouth; I smile over his kisses. He wraps his arms around me and I start to feel him harden underneath.

"What?" He whispers. I shake my head slightly.

"Nothing, you are just so damn hot."

He chuckles and looks at me admiringly, "Well, you are absolutely breath-taking."

He makes me feel so sexy, but nervous, do I tell him this is my first time? No, I don't want to be a buzz kill. This time when we kiss each other it seems to be more urgent and wanting, buzzing with anticipation, feeling his strong arms hold me, wanting him to touch me everywhere. He plants soft kisses down my neck. Feeling his rough stubble on my skin sends shivers of excitement through my body, I need him closer, I want him. I can tell how much he wants this by the way he pushes against me. I feel him even more now and see the desire in his eyes. I tease my fingers against him.

It's like a swimming pool down in the knicker regions, I am soaked. I have never felt so turned on by anyone in my life. I slowly unbutton his shirt, never leaving his lips, and he grabs my hand to stop.

"What are you doing?" He whispers, I look at him a little shyly. "Is that what you want?" He continues.

"Yes, I want you. You don't know how long I have waited for this moment."

"I have thought of little else, so yes I do."

He releases his grip on my hand and I continue to take off his shirt. He eases out of it slowly to reveal his toned chest and it's everything, everything I fantasised about. I can't help but run my hands down his chiselled, god-like chest. I trace his chest, nipples and abs with my fingertips, committing this to memory and his eyes close slowly.

Just any excuse to touch him, his skin is warm and soft to the touch. I arch over and kiss him across his chest, feeling his breath deepen, showing me, he is enjoying it. I run my tongue along his nipples and suck gently on them, feeling his naked skin against my lips feels amazing.

I quickly take off my top and throw it on the floor, sitting in my bra, I feel a little shy as I have never really been naked in front of anyone and I am glad of the low light from the lamp. But he makes me forget almost instantly as the tips of his fingers caress me slowly down my cheek, along my collarbone, across my chest and to my breast. Pleasure prickles my skin where his fingertips have touched. He pulls me closer, stroking my arms tenderly, and then grabs each side of my waist pulling me in. He slowly peels back my bra and swirls his tongue over my nipple, making them hard and wanting, whilst attempting to unhook the bra.

After a few seconds, I let out a little giggle and push his hands away and do it myself. He looks up at me and smiles awkwardly in relief. He cups both my breasts into his hands and trails his tongue lightly over each side. I lean my head back and let out a quiet moan. I can feel him beneath me even more so now and panic sets in, this is really happening. He pulls me off him in one swift movement and lays me gently on the sofa.

He gazes at me momentarily, then his tongue is hot on my skin, I feel my heart beating with the pleasure of having that skin-to-skin contact. I like that he is starting to take control now. Trailing slow, soft kisses down, lower and lower, I arch my back up as he starts to pull down my jeans and knickers in one go and I have never felt so exposed, turned on and nervous in one go, ever. He moans slightly with excitement brushing his lips gently all the way down my thigh.

"You are the most beautiful woman I have ever seen," he murmurs as he kisses me, carefully making his way back up to my sensitive area, and then his tongue is on me, which makes me gasp in delight. He is sucking and licking, it feels wet and a bit weird but oddly satisfying. He thrusts his tongue inside and I suck in a ragged breath, sigh contently, then groan with pleasure, greedy for more. I feel pressure and his then finger enters me, which makes me gasp again. Definitely did not see that coming so soon, he seems eager. His fingers are heavy and clumsy against my insides and I wince a bit, I put my hand over his.

"Not so rough," I tell him. It all feels new, being touched down there by someone other than myself. I feel tense and try my best to enjoy it, to enjoy him, people say oral is one of the best bits, but as I have nothing to compare it with, I am not sure this is for me.

"Sorry," he murmurs and then his tongue is at my entrance again. Licking and sucking, his rough tongue feels intense against my clit.

But then he starts twisting his fingers inside and I tense. Does he even know what he is doing? I put my hand on him again, and he slowly retreats, definitely not a skill he has mastered, but something to work on. He removes his fingers to the outside massaging my sensitive nub with his thumb and he slowly kisses up my body, wipes his mouth with the back of his hand and kisses me on the lips. I am not sure if that is the most disgusting thing ever or a massive turn-on.

I will bank that and decide on that later, too.

I move my hands and start fumbling with the button on his trousers, which I expertly get off. So here I am, naked, him in his boxers. The kisses are slow, deep and tender and I am unsure at this moment where he begins and I end. I slip my hand into his boxers and I hear him hitch his breath. I take him into my hand, surprised at how hard, soft and hairy it is in one go. Unsure how to touch him, or what he likes, I go with what I have seen on porn channels and debate whether I should put it in my mouth and what it might taste of. Feeling a bit empowered and sexy I slowly slide my hand up and down against him.

He lets out a groan, so I take that as a good sign.

I continue holding him, making the movements slowly but firmly, he feels big. Then after a few moments, he lets out a ragged breath and I feel a warm and sticky mess on my hand. He looks at me slightly surprised and a little embarrassed.

"I'm too excited, you turn me on so much. It's embarrassing," he blurts out. I can't help but throw him a half laugh, half smile.

"Glad I'm not the only one."

He sits up, I offer him some tissues from the side table and he cleans himself up. He looks at me sheepishly, I feel a little disappointed and he gets up and walks away from the front room. I watch him as his broad shoulders and his sexy arse sway into the other room. Do I put my clothes back on? I sit there for a few moments and then decide that sitting in the front room naked is weird, so I get up and fish out my clothes from the floor.

"What are you doing?" he asks as he returns.

Feeling a little bit embarrassed as I watch him, boxers off and his naked body moving towards me. Male genitals are weird-looking, like a stuffed sock gone wrong. A real-life hard-on, a fully erect penis, what a great name. I can't help but stare as it points at me.

Half excited, half terrified.

But before I can answer he crashes back into my lips with a feverish kiss. My mind is blurry, I can't form words, and I am lost in him. My stomach lurches in delight as he pins me against the wall with both his hands beside my head.

His urgency, his need, his want, as his hands roam my body, it's intoxicating. I smooth my hands around his toned body, wanting that closeness again. He lifts me up like I weigh nothing, and I giggle a little as he manoeuvres us both back to the sofa. Effortlessly he eases me back down. He lowers himself on top, I gasp at the feeling of both our naked bodies together. It's a sexual and intimate feeling and I relish the contact, it's such a turn-on. As he kisses me again, I release a small moan as his tongue thrusts deeper into my mouth, and I arch my mouth for that deeper intimacy, desperate for him there, desperate for him inside me. I have never wanted anyone so much; the anticipation is torture. If he doesn't do it now, I might explode with sexual frustration. Plus, I am that wet I may slide off the flipping sofa. We both come up for air, he grabs a condom and starts to put it on. I feel nervous again.

"Can you pinch the top?" I do as he says, confused. "If there's air in it, it can break," he says with certainty, as if it has happened to him before because he's slept with many girls, which makes me feel sad for a moment. He slowly positions himself between my legs, I feel the tip just in and I clench with uncertainty. "Say you want me, Cora, say you want this."

"I want this, Zach, but go slow, okay?" He seems unsure by my words, or has he changed his mind?

I hold my breath in anticipation.

He nudges slowly inside me, his breath shaky as if he is feeling my nerves and I start to panic a little, this is not a sexy mood to be in. The V card is going, now, this is not the wrong decision, we want each other. He slowly inches in, the burning and stretching make me gasp and I cry out as my body adjusts to his size. His gaze never wavers. He looks at me as if he wants to see all of me and it is the hottest thing I have ever seen. He strokes the side of my face as he hovers above me.

"Are you okay?" I nod. "We can stop anytime you want." I wrap my arms around his back, feeling the weight above me, his powerful muscles, pinning me down into a wonderful feeling of sexual awakening. Although I quickly check he's in the right hole because it does feel like he is moving against my arse. Nope, definitely right hole. I didn't expect it to be this uncomfortable. But just his gaze and the want I feel make me relax more, forgetting the rest of the world exists and we just see each other. The way it was meant to be, from the beginning.

"Don't stop." He smirks and sets a slow and steady pace, rotating his hips, which I appreciate. I start to relax further, feeling less tense. I hear his breath heavy against my ear as he whispers my name and sweet words of how beautiful I am, sending a shiver down my body.

His breathing is so loud in my ear. I close my eyes tight, trying to relax even more and it makes me think about how I act just before I get a jab at the doctors, which is such a weird thing to consider whilst I am having sex with the hottest man ever. He starts to move a little faster and deeper to the point it makes me gasp again, our hips meet in perfect rhythm, our bodies together and pleasure surges through me, he is inside me, we are really doing this! His hips move more frantically, and I feel him start to unravel as his breathing becomes harder against my shoulder.

"I'm... I'm going to cum," he shudders, groans with pleasure and sighs, I feel him pulse inside me and then we melt into one another as his body collapses on me in a sweaty satisfied mess.

Well, he is satisfied, I am unsure.

Even though it was an amazing first experience, the V card has gone, it was slightly disappointing. Friends have spoken about orgasms, but I don't think I had one. Is that normal? His weight sags on top of me and he holds me close for a moment and then pulls out, grabbing more tissue and thrusting some at me. Which I realise I need as soon as I sit up as my opening is wet and there is a lot of sweat. I look down with a furrowed brow, again unsure if this is disgusting or sexy, another thing I need to talk to Sophie about. He leans over, cups my face and kisses me gently on the lips.

"Thank you."

Thank you. What is this, a service? Erm, you're not welcome.

Seventeen

The second time – Zach

E ejit, that came out wrong, it sounded perfect in my head but came out so, so wrong.

"You are amazing," I add. I need to work on my smooth talking.

I look down and there is a small, red stain on the blanket. "Erm, I don't want to be rude, but was that your first time?" She looks at me horrified; I look down to show her what I mean. She nods, grabs more tissue from the side and starts to wipe down the mess. I search her face and I can see that there are a lot of thoughts going through her mind.

"Does that change anything if it was?" She whispers, not daring to look up.

I cup her face, forcing her to look at me. "No, but I would suggest visiting a doctor if it wasn't." She half-heartedly smiles. Well, I thought it was funny, but I seem to be coming off as a bit of an arse in her eyes. It is surprising that she was a virgin. She is so beautiful and intelligent. She doesn't seem to be the type that sleeps around, even when all that shit with Stefan came out.

That was a difficult pill to swallow. There were so many rumours and overheard conversations, that I decided to step back and try not to listen. I was never that guy who involved himself in gossip tripe, but it stung a wee bit. I guess the rumours weren't true then, and even though I did believe her, I am relieved. I never even thought I would be her first. I mean, I am honoured she chose me, although saying that, she was my second.

A wave of anxiety starts to appear in my stomach.

I haven't had sex since Sarah and it's not as if I have had the time to be getting my dick wet at every opportunity. I have been a busy boy. I only slept with her twice, but that was years ago. This might as well have been my first time all over again, for how long it has been. I don't feel porn and a tissue really counts. I don't feel I did a bad job, she seemed to be enjoying herself, and I know I was. I double-check for any breakages and then discard the condom and put my clothes back on. I pull the blanket off the sofa and put it in the wash for her. It's the least I could do. When I return back to the front room, she is staring at a family photo. She is fully clothed too, which I am slightly disappointed by. I would happily do it all again if she wanted.

I wrap my arms around her from behind and gently kiss her neck. She puts the photo down and I wonder if the other rumours I heard were true about her mum. But I won't ask about it unless she tells me. She holds her hand over mine and twists around and nuzzles into my neck. I inhale into her hair. So, this is what content feels like. It has been a while.

"I regret nothing and I feel really special that you let me be your first," I whisper, which was the truth. I wanted to be in the here and now. Tomorrow was another day, I would face the music then, if I had to. I sit back down on the sofa and she follows me. I lie down and she joins me, moulding her body next to mine with her head in the cruck of my arm. I hold her close and stroke her hair, inhaling her tropical shampoo scent. She pulls another blanket over us both and we settle in to watch re-runs of *Friends*.

I wake a few hours later and see that dawn has reared its ugly head. I look down at Cora, who is sleeping peacefully. I am tempted to wake her and tell her I need to go, but then I think of the night she had, she probably needs the rest.

I inhale into her hair again, trying to memorise it. She smells fantastic, like the summer when rain has fallen and all the flowers come into bloom. I like it, I like her a lot, she feels like home. I can tell I am falling for her, and I like that feeling too, I don't want it to stop.

I want to stay like this forever, away from the outside world, away from the drama, and it would just be me and her. But then I hear a car drive by and the crash of reality hits me like a steam train. I can never be hers; she can never be mine and I shouldn't be here.

I should never have come.

I carefully ease myself out of her hold, she stirs a wee bit, but her breathing evens out and I knew I haven't woken her, which I am surprisingly pleased about. It's the morning after and even though I wanted this to happen, I feel the awkwardness.

What would she say? What would I say? I still do not have any regrets, but I didn't want her to have any either. However, the consequences of our actions and my actions were starting to pile on my shoulders. I decide a note would be best, I don't want to leave without saying or doing anything, I don't want to be a shit about this. I crept around, gathering my stuff quickly. It was a Friday, but an inset day at school and most of the staff had to go in for some training or another but because I had put some extra hours in for Governor's meetings and twilights, I actually had a Friday off for once. What do I say in the note...

Had to get home, and didn't want to wake you, Z x

It would have to do, I don't have to go home, but I don't want to stay either. I feel uneasy and a little scared in case she regrets what happened, or maybe someone would see.

If I left early, it would be our little secret, but then I feel bad, as I don't want it to be a secret, it feels wrong. Conflicted, I leave the note stood up on the coffee table and let myself out the front door, closing it quietly behind me. I realise I only live a 15-minute drive from her house, which seems so odd, to be so close to her and never know. I hope no one finds out I raided the office files last night for her address. That is a serious GDPR issues and a sackable offence, but my brain went into overdrive, remembering when my mum got sick and how desperate I was in need of that comfort and reassurance. I knew I never wanted Cora to feel like she had to confront this alone, and it only made me even more determined to see her after the way she looked at me before she climbed into the ambulance.

So alone, so afraid, my heart broke a wee bit for her. I wanted to be there for her, I wanted to be that comfort. But now, now I need to get the hell out of here and have a shower and a shave.

As soon as I arrive home and take a shower, I explode with guilt. Moving away from the situation, what we did starts to settle in my mind. Knowing what I have done is so wrong, my brain starts to think of what kind of trouble I would be in if anyone found out! It starts to circle around my head like an eagle in prey mode, 'round and 'round it goes. It feels as if my head is going to implode.

I could not sort my thoughts out. If someone did find out, I would never teach again. What is wrong with me?

Why would I jeopardise my future for a woman?

A woman that I teach, and oh shit, I am definitely going to prison. What if she tells someone? What if someone did see me? What if I accidentally slip and tell someone? Is that a jail sentence, of five years? What example am I setting as a person?

But another voice starts to filter in with a slight bit of reason.

She is a consenting adult. I really like her, she is different, funny, and beautiful. I enjoy talking to her, and being in her company, she makes me feel good about myself, like I am a good person and that I deserve happiness, that I deserve happiness with her. This isn't just a hump-and-dump session, I want to be with her and that makes things complicated, so, so complicated. I check my phone just after lunch to see if she has texted, but there is nothing.

Maybe she does regret it.

I keep myself busy, planning for the next half term and sorting my to-do list with the school. With A-level exams starting in only a few weeks, I need to be ready, but then that would be the last week I would teach her.

I groan.

I thought maybe giving into this tension, this lust and want, and sleeping with her, would get her off my mind. That getting my fix would get her out of my system, that I would feel satisfied and get my thoughts out of the gutter. But it's made me want her more, it's made me want to explore what we have. I knew that once would never be enough, how is that even possible? What the hell is wrong with me? I am a grown-arse man, I am not meant to fall for these temptations, I am not supposed to give into my lust.

A few hours later, an email comes through from the deputy explaining everything that had happened with her dad and with an update on his condition. He is going into surgery today, and could people send some pennies as they want to send flowers. As if flowers would help him get better. I decide early evening that I will go for a run, to disperse this nervous energy. But what I really want to know is what she is thinking.

Was she disappointed? Did she want me? I felt selfish with my thoughts, as she must be going out of her mind about her dad, but I couldn't stop. She had made it clearly evident she wanted me before. And since the Stefan thing, she had stayed out of my way and I thought I would be happy about it, relieved even. But it made me even more worked up, it made it worse for me. She'd missed a few lessons last week (due to illness according to the register) and even in the classes she did attend, she sat with her head down and would leave as soon as the bell went. She was definitely making herself unseen.

I decide halfway through my run that I will run past her house 'accidentally' and see if she is in. I don't know if she will be in or what to expect but I want to see if she is doing okay.

Just after 9 pm, I run the long route and slowly jog by her house, like a creeper in the dark. I keep to the other side of the road, under the cover of the trees and pull my hoodie up, in case someone sees me, and I have a justifiable excuse for being in this neighbourhood.

As I approach her house, the lights are on. My heart skips a beat. Maybe I should have texted her, perhaps she wants nothing to do with me. Or maybe I can go in and we can talk? As I approach the house, I see in the window that someone is with her, which makes me angry and sad. But then I realise it's that Sophie girl from my music class and I let out a sigh of relief.

Then I'm mad again at myself, why the hell have I come back, eejit! I sprint away as quickly as I can, realising that I am being an absolutely needy prat and run home thinking someone could have seen me again. I need to go home and drink a lot of beers and try to forget her.

Failing miserably.

Eighteen

The morning after — Cora

Sophie came by in the evening to check on me, and I felt relieved to talk to someone about what happened with Dad. His surgery had gone well, but all this waiting around had driven me to another level of craziness in my head and sent me into a spiral of panic. Sophie made me shower; we ordered takeout and then went over every detail of the last two days. It made me feel calmer about it. But Zach, that felt like it was a dream, or it had happened to another person. I had to talk to someone about it, that was a whole different experience. Even though she did not know it was him, I had to vocalise it and validate it, even. We have become closer over the last few months, and it has killed me not to be truthful to her. Withholding secrets is hard for me in general, I am not a great liar and always wear my emotions on my face. People always know if I am happy or sad, so I was doing a great job of acting; she had no idea yet.

Did I trust her enough to keep it secret? Honestly, the answer was no.

It made me sad that I felt like that, but maybe I also did not want to tell her, as she would tell me I was stupid for wanting him. Or that by telling her, it was no longer a secret, or even real. No, my reasons for not telling her who it was, were justified, but I did want to say to her that I had sex.

"So how did you find it?" She smirks, shoveling crisps into her mouth. I look at her, deadpan. "What? I am PMSing and I need the crappy food to make me feel better. So… dish."

"It was uncomfortable and weird. I feel sore, very sore."

She laughs. "Totally normal. You are being broken in."

"That sounds absolutely disgusting, who says that?"

"Everyone says that, but it's true, you are. Like shoes, you need to wear them several times before they feel comfortable and then you enjoy wearing them." I laugh. Who compares losing their virginity to wearing in shoes? "Are you sure this is what you wanted?" She continues. "I thought you were trying to avoid Mr Married Man because you know… it's wrong?"

"I know, but he was here and being so nice, and yes, I was trying to avoid him, but still, he is hot, and I wanted him so much!"

"Look at the dreamy look in your eyes! You are a lucky bitch. At least you got some. You know, they did this whole scientific experiment. Apparently, when women have sex, they release this extra hormone or something and then they feel like they are in love or bonded for life."

"Serious?" I close my eyes. I feel that it's true. If I felt consumed before, I feel brainwashed by him now and I swear I can still smell him. A mint and citrus aroma, it's now my favourite smell. I shouldn't have fallen asleep last night; I should have begged him to stay and make babies with me! Beautiful Zach babies. My thoughts are racing a mile a second. "What if I didn't measure up to his standards, or he saw my panic and I did something wrong?" Maybe that is why he hasn't messaged me.

"Nah, you can't have done anything wrong, he's a man, he got his dick wet with a sexy hot girl, and he doesn't give one shit Cee Cee."

"Really?"

"Did he cum?"

"Yeah."

"Then don't sweat it; he had a great time. So how big was the man-penis, the schlong, the willy, the beast, the sausage roll?" I laugh.

"It was pretty big."

We gossip and catch up, and it feels really nice. We watch *The Greatest Showman* on the flat screen. Even the lovers in that film feel they can't be together, but in the end, they are because love overcomes all. I inwardly sigh. Can we overcome our obstacles to be together? Does he want to be with me? I look at my phone for the millionth time and he still hasn't texted me, my high of being with him is now becoming super low.

Just before midnight, Sophie leaves. Daisy is still at the hospital and I lie in bed that night, alone, going over the horrible day at the hospital. Dad is now recovering in ICU, and they said he should be home within the next week or two, which is a relief.

But I still can't sleep.

If I can get to sleep in two hours, I will have five hours of sleep, I am trying to bargain with my brain at 2:30 am. I have tried to count sheep, listen to calming music, and I try a bit of meditation and mindfulness, and they are all giving me the middle finger for no sleep tonight.

Where are the sleeping tablets when I need them?

I want to feel rested and I want everything to be okay. But it's not. The short sleep I do have is filled with insane and confusing dreams, just like my daily life.

The reoccurring one is about me.

I am walking into a room and the people in there stop talking, all eyes are on me, and the people start running towards me. Every bone in my body is screaming at me, I am running but it's never fast enough. I wake up in a panic and covered in a cold sweat.

The night terrors have started again!

Nineteen

As time goes by — Cora

During the Easter holidays, I heard not one word from Zach, which made me feel that sleeping together was the biggest mistake. Even though I pretty much threw myself at him, he wanted this as much as I did. Why have sex with me if he wouldn't even talk to me? And to hell if I am going to text him first.

But the silent treatment, the silence was making my heart ache. It made a big gap in my head of unanswered questions. Then I filled it in with my overactive imagination telling myself I wasn't good enough, that I was too ugly, or too fat or that he regretted it, or maybe his cagy personality was because he really was seeing someone else.

Was that his thing? Had he slept with other students, was he seeing other girls? I felt used and I even thought of driving over there and confronting him. I even drove past his house a few times, but I really was going crazy and felt like a stalker, like an idiot. So, I banned myself from my car.

After the first week of moping, I threw myself into my revision. I clean the house and I lie in my bed watching *Netflix*, crying at the stupidest things. One evening, Sophie burst into my room and told me we were going swimming.

"Come on, you have been in your house all week or at the hospital. I haven't seen you and your dad gets out tomorrow, so you will be all over that, so I won't see you again until we go back to school. And I was hoping you could come and swim with me and see the new lifeguard. Cee Cee, he is so fit, my vagina's going to explode."

I smile at her but then pull a serious face. "Sophie, I would rather stick forks in my eyes than go swimming."

She gives me the pouty mouth and the puppy-dog eyes. "Pleeeeeease, they have a sauna and jacuzzi, they had a whole refurb in the swim bit over Christmas, it looks amazeballs. The leisure centre is the only thing this town has going for it, apart from underage drinking, and I can't go there on my own, because that's like social suicide. Pleaaaaaaaaase!"

"So, actually, I don't need to swim."

"No, you can sit there, cute as fuck in your bikini and your tan, whilst I fake an almost-drown. Then the fit lifeguard can jump into the pool and save me, give me mouth-to-mouth resuscitation whilst I touch his abs."

She made me belly laugh, which was nice as I had not laughed in a while and then I felt sad. My dad almost dies, and I sit here moping and moaning about a bloody guy when I need to be up and grabbing life by the horns. I need to get out of this bedroom, out of this house and get back out into the real world. Starting by going swimming but shaving first because I cannot remember when I did that last and that would also be a furry disaster.

We arrive at the leisure centre about an hour later and Sophie is buzzing with excitement. I change into my deep green bikini; this one has a plunge bra, so the girls look bouncy and perky whilst the back of it hugs my bum, and I do look nice in it. We enter the swimming pool area and I am glad that it's not too busy; Sophie grabs my hand and whispers.

"Holy shit, he looks even better at night, it must be a full moon; look at him Cee Cee."

I turn to look at the lifeguard sitting lazily in his chair, and she is not wrong, he is pretty good-looking. He's got that cute geeky look, where he has those large glasses, and floppy sandy blonde hair, with a strong chin and a sparkle in his eye. He runs a hand through his hair and surveys the room, landing on Sophie and myself checking him out. He gives us both a small smile and a nod as if we know him and enjoys us dribbling over his face. I leave Sophie to continue to ogle and make my way over to the steam room.

It's empty and I am pleased.

I lie down on the hot tiled seat and take deep breaths, feeling the warm air soak into my body and start to relieve some of the tension I did not know I was holding. After several minutes, I am feeling a little bit too hot. So, I wander over to the jacuzzi area. I glance around and see that Sophie is talking to the lifeguard – that girl does not waste her time. I lower myself in, enjoy the warm bubbly sensation it offers, and lean back, closing my eyes and, for a moment, I relax.

"Well, I did not expect to see you here, are you following me?" I open one eye, and close it again, inwardly groaning at why I hate living in such a small town.

"What do you want, Stefan?" I ensure I keep my eyes closed as making any contact with the dickhead will definitely give him the wrong idea. Did I mention he is a dickhead?

"Rude."

"Not rude. Rude is spreading lies about someone else and making up shit to make yourself look good." I yawn to make the point that this is a boring conversation and he is a boring dickhead. I open my eyes as it's silent and he's just glowering at me with thunder in his eyes; then something flashes over his face and he smirks. I roll my eyes. This is pathetic.

"How's Daisy?"

I eye him cautiously. What does that even mean?

"Why?"

"Just wondering."

"Don't go near my sister, you little psychopath."

He smirks again, closing his eyes and leaning back into the jacuzzi. Sophie approaches, looking super upset.

"Cee Cee, I just found an eyelash extension floating in the pool and it nearly went in my mouth and…" She stops talking and realises Stefan is in the jacuzzi and we are having some odd stand-off. "Can we go, please?" I stand and get out quickly but notice Stefan opening his eyes slightly, giving me the once over, and it makes me feel naked and dirty. "Everything okay?" Sophie asks as we walk back to the changing room.

"Yeah, that was just… weird. How did it go with the fit lifeguard guy?"

She pouts. "He has a boyfriend. Of course, he does; everyone has a bloody boyfriend except me."

After another shitty night's sleep, I wake up and literally down a whole cafetière of coffee because nothing will darken my mood today as Dad is coming home. I am determined to be positive. I clean the house from top to bottom and ensure that everything is tidy and ready for Dad's return. A community ambulance arrives just after lunch and it's an utter relief, I cannot describe how good it is to have him back in the house.

He's my calm, without him, who am I? I am no one.

I know he's still unwell and he has been in bed all day, but he is here, he is home. A fantastic company turned up early this morning and installed a bed in the office downstairs for a month. This way, he doesn't have to climb the stairs, in the hope that he has a speedier recovery. He can slowly get about; he uses a stick to help him get to the toilet and back, but he tires quickly and still needs lots of rest. Apparently, in a few more weeks, we should see more of an improvement and a physio will come every day as well to help him move around more. I try not to hover or be a pain, but I check in on him hourly, and he seems to be getting annoyed. I am scared that if I leave him any longer, I might find him dead in his bed, morbid, I know, but when he passed out in his office, something switched in my head. I keep replaying it over and over.

Was there more I could have done? What would have happened if I hadn't been there? Would he have died? These thoughts constantly plague me night and day, and sleeping has become an even bigger nightmare. When I close my eyes now, my dreams bring me back to the office, and I can never get to him in time. He always dies, and it has had me on edge. After a few days of this, I think something snaps in Dad.

"Cora, enough!" He barks, his tone and sharpness stopping me from fluffing his pillows. He pauses, and his face softens. "I am okay darling; you do not need to do this."

"I want to."

"No, you don't, I am okay, come here." He pats the side of the bed, and he gestures for a cuddle. I sit down next to him and he cuddles me close. "I love you very much and I am okay. The doctor says I will recover, so stop fussing and go out. It's the Friday night before your exams start, go let off steam. I know how hard you have been working."

Tears roll down my face, and I wipe them away quickly. "I can't leave you; I don't want to."

"Cora," he looks at me with his tired eyes. "When it is meant to be and it is my time, there is nothing that you or I can do about it. I have had a nice life, we have a good family, with love and laughter and that's all I can ask for..." he reflects for a moment. "So, no amount of fussing will help. I know you love me and you are such a caring young lady, but do not burden yourself with this, and I will text, ring or shout if I need help. But for now, just let me rest and go and study, or go out with your friends, or whatever it is you teenagers do nowadays."

I hold him close for a while and he eventually dozes off. I slip out of the bedroom quietly, unable to control the tears any longer. My dad is the best dad I can ask for. I need to be strong for him whilst he gets better, but now I am going to hide in my bed and cry, because at the moment that is what I do best.

Twenty

Totally off my game – Cora

It's the Monday after the Easter break and three weeks since the one-to-one with Mr Jones at my house. I still feel really hurt he left without saying goodbye, I still have the thought that maybe it was disappointing sex for him and he needed to leave.

That was what I was telling myself.

Today, I am having the worst period ever, of course, because this week was the week of my A-level music examinations. He hasn't texted and my mood has gone from an anxiety-ridden mess to utter depression. I miss him so much. I am so angry with these thoughts and I also want to rip his head off – thanks again mother nature, and your hormones can suck it! I had never really wanted to have sex with anyone until I met Zach, and now, now he hasn't spoken to me, and honestly, I feel used.

I also feel I've changed.

With the shock of Dad having a heart attack and me losing my V card, I have changed. I feel different. Like my innocence has been taken, but everyone, everyone else is still the same. I don't feel like I am an introvert, but I have totally gone back into my tortoise shell and am hiding from the world. If I hide, then the pain might go away or miss me out next time on its rounds. I had stuck to my plan of staying away – luckily two weeks of that were Easter holidays so I threw myself into practising, seeing Dad and helping him recover at home. Plus, I had also decided that actually, no man was going to dictate my life.

He didn't text me; I was hurt but it was okay.

I did not need him to make me feel better, he was not interested any-more, and I had to be okay with that.

I WILL be okay with that.

I had successfully ignored and avoided Zach the first week back, and he seemed to have a constant gloom in his eyes. During the mock exams, he had tried to ask a lot of class questions, some directed at me, but I gave simple answers and reverted back to one of my classmates, and this seemed to piss him off. I knew it was a stupid game, but I had given up on us, and so I decided I would just be a normal, shitty teenager towards him, my teacher, because I know I meant nothing to him.

That's what I told myself, again.

But now the examinations are here, a whole week with Mr Hottie, and I feel like a greased-up wet wipe, stomach cramps, the whole thing. Thanks, mother nature, I love you too, bitch. My thoughts trail to Dad. Even though his operation was a success two weeks prior, he still looks so frail and helpless. This week already is feeling pretty rubbish and it's only 9 am, Monday morning.

"Cora, you need to focus, the deadline to submit this piece is on Friday." I glance up at Zach, noticing his furrowed, sexy brow. It seems that he's not the only one stressed this week. However rough I feel, being close to him feels so good again. It just feels right, and those three weeks of man-hating him disappear. I thought if I just avoid the elephant in the room (sex), we can just carry on like normal, because if he doesn't want to talk about how awful I was, then I am super happy to gloss over the situation as well.

"Right, sorry."

I turn back to amend some notes on the music sheet, but then my mind starts to wonder again about Dad. He always seemed so fit and healthy, he never had problems before. Is this a family gene thing? And it made me wonder about my mum, not that I gave her much thought anymore, but Dad NEVER talks about her. I could visit her.

And give her the satisfaction that I cared? No, thanks!

Sure, I had questions about her when I was younger, but all I got was they were madly in love, she became pregnant unexpectedly quickly, that both Daisy and I came out perfect, and then she had to leave.

How they met wasn't much clearer, why she left was a mystery, and why she disappeared and reappeared was treated as the norm. How she became so dependent on the drink was never addressed, and when she went to prison, we never spoke about it. But I wanted answers, I needed answers. Whenever I asked Dad:

"How did you meet?"

"Through a friend," he would reply.

"Which friend?" I badgered.

"I can't remember now, honey, it was so long ago. It doesn't do well to dwell in the past when you have such a brilliant future ahead of you." His voice was soft, but it always seemed to pain him when I asked, so I stopped asking. I feel guilty for asking, but what if he dies? Then I will never have any answers. He was, is, such a great Dad, and it always makes me feel bad when he has that broken-hearted look in his eyes. Mum did that to him. He thinks I don't see it, but I do, I see the pain behind his eyes. Is it pain from mum leaving? I desperately want to know the truth, but at what cost?

"Okay, what is it?" I look back up at Zach.

"What's what?" I eye him curiously.

"You have been glazing over for the last half an hour. Do we need to reschedule... do we need to talk?"

He sighs heavily and puts the equipment down and pulls his chair forward. Oh no, is this the part where he tells me that the sex was crap and he wants nothing to do with me?

"Clearly, we are not going to get the piece done unless we talk about whatever it is that is bothering you. Please tell me what is on your mind. Is it what happened between us?" I shake my head; I don't want to hear it, or his pity. "Look, I am sorry I didn't text... I thought about calling, but I was unsure what to say... I just wanted our next conversation to be in person... we both know this can't go any further; it can't happen again, it-" I put my hand up to stop him from talking. I don't need his excuses, either.

"-It was a mistake." I can't keep the hurt from my voice. I knew what he was going to say. His eyebrows shoot up.

"No, no," he replies kindly, "Not a mistake... I don't think that. I don't think that at all. Do you think it was a mistake?"

I shake my head slightly; his gaze is deep and unwavering. I am shocked he doesn't think it was a mistake and relieved, but now I am even more confused. I want him to open up, be true and tell me how he really feels, tell me he wants me, tell me this won't end. But even in my head, I know he won't do any of those things, and my heart sinks. It will never work when he is so guarded.

I want everything from him, I want him to love the idea of us, but he does not, he will not. Nevertheless, he has apologised, and he doesn't think it was a mistake, which also makes my heart soar.

I feel I owe him something as he was so honest with me several weeks back about his mum, and who else have I got to talk to at the moment? I think Sophie has had enough drama from me to last a lifetime and, in turn, she has been avoiding me these last few weeks. Daisy can do one, she's a loose cannon on her best day and Dad, well, he needs no stress, he doesn't need mine.

"Are you sure you want to hear this, the inner mind of such a teenager?" He rolls his eyes and smirks, a little amused. To kiss that smirk...

"You are an intelligent woman, Cora, I am sure whatever it is you need to talk about is not as bad as you think." He gazes at me intently, clearly wanting to help, but is this another line that I don't want to cross? Yes, we had sex, but I have tried every which way to make sure I seem unavailable to him this last week.

But he has also done the same, and look where that's got me, nowhere, and this would be emotional reliance, wouldn't it? I mean, if he cares about me, surely, I can talk about problems or even receive a text from him?

But neither of these things happened.

I take a deep breath, ignore my overwhelming thoughts and decide to bare my soul.

"Have you ever felt where things are good in your life, then a horrific incident makes you question everything about life?"

"I am assuming we are talking about your Dad's heart attack?" I nod.

"I guess what I am trying to say is... if he dies... my sister, and me, we will be on our own, we have no other family, Dad was an only child. My mum isn't someone we can count on... I just feel so lost and helpless." He absorbs what I have said and thinks for a minute.

"In my short life, I have found that I may not be able to choose my family, but I can choose my friends, who I feel can be an extension of a family.

Friends can become family. Cora, you will never be alone, not really. You will always have him with you and your mum, too, in some way. I believe that parents never truly leave us, they live on in you."

"I am pretty sure that you have stolen that quote from *The Lion King*."

He smiles. He's so gorgeous when he smiles, he lights up the room. "That may be true, however, a good *Disney* movie can never steer someone wrong with good advice in a crisis."

"I didn't peg you as a *Disney* fan?"

"Yes... well." He shifts uncomfortably, embarrassed by the remark, cute. "What I mean is, it's okay to feel anxious when things like this happen. Your dad is recovering well I hear?" I nod.

He continues, "I remember when my mum was diagnosed with cancer, it was touch and go for a few years until she got a final diagnosis of terminal. And I remember going through all the emotions, and it was a struggle, but everyone learns to deal with it in their own way, and that is okay too."

"When did you get so smart?"

"It's that four-year age gap, I swear."

Flirty.

I laugh and he laughs, I love that laugh, feeling the weight of the world slowly lifting. "Look, I have something for you." He pulls out a tattered book from his shelf. I look at it closely, *The Grief We're Given, Poems by William Bortz*. I look back at him, confused.

"Read it, there will be a poem in there for you, somewhere. It will give you what you need, to know you are not alone, and that you are not the only one who feels this way. That someone else shares your pain... it really helped me when my mum got sick. It opens up so many doors on grief, and relationships, it helps to find an answer or some solace. It will make you slow down and process your thoughts. Poetry, I think, helps to put words to feelings you can't quite say yet." Even when I feel like the darkness of my thoughts has crept in, he shines a big-ass torch on it to show that there's still light.

"How do you do that?" I whisper.

"Do what?"

"Make everything feel like it's going to be okay."

"It is going to be okay, Cora, you are so beautiful, how can I not want to make you smile?" He realises what he has said and looks taken aback. He clears his throat. "I mean... I always want to make sure all my students are well mentally, you know... with exams coming up, everyone needs to be focused 100% and on top of their game."

I beam at him with a full cheesy smile. "You think I am beautiful?" We stare at one another for a few moments. "Well, now I am definitely ready to get back to this." I see a twitch of his jaw like he is suppressing a smile. I push away my feelings, and over the next few hours, I play my piano piece.

When I finish my piece, he plays it back with a sparkle in his eye. He is pretty hot when he gets excited. I see his musical passion just oozing out of him, and I see why he makes such a good teacher – when you look past the sex god. Although, with his intense stares, we are pretty much having sex with our eyes. Working through the keys, he helps with some of the off notes, moving his finger over mine and finding any way to touch me, which I am not complaining about, but it does make it difficult to concentrate.

"Cora, this is amazing. I honestly think this is A-grade work, you should be really proud of yourself. You were not wrong when you said about bringing the passion and feeling alive during your music, it definitely made me smile."

"You remember that?"

"I remember everything you say," he mumbles back and I avert my eyes as he reveals this.

"I don't know whether to be worried or excited by that."

He looks uncomfortable again, but his deep, brown eyes roam my face. "Are you ready to record the words?" This makes my stomach flip because I wrote it about him, and I am unsure how he will take it. Cheesy and a little childish? But singing is my outlet and these last several weeks it has been the only thing that has got me through, trying not to lose my mind, wanting to be near him but unable to. I want to show him how I feel.

This is what I want, I can do this.

Although I would rather die than tell him how crazy I am about him, I thought maybe if I wrote it in a song, it made me sound less crazy, more grown-up. I take a deep breath as anxiety swirls in my stomach and I nod.

He moves his hands quickly over the dials, setting the music up through to the booth, and it whirls into motion once again. I put on the headphones and listen to my music play. I close my eyes and begin to sing.

You are perfect for me, since the day we met, everything felt so right, I see only you and I know that you see me, you're all that I need, the reason why I smile, you are the reason why I breathe,

But you are all that I want when it comes to being with you, no matter where we have come from, no matter where we go, it will always be you,

When the skies are dark and grey and all the doors are closed, the rising of the tied makes it hard to breathe, I see you and you take my hand to stop the tears from falling, I have found you next to me,

But you are all that I want when it comes to being with you, no matter where we have come from, no matter where we go, it will always be you,

I know you, you are my light, you are brighter than the moon, brighter than the star, you are my light, please don't ever change,

I will wait for you, until the end of time, my love, my heart believed I would find you, a chance meeting brought your heart to me, a brand-new life for us is down the road waiting, I am waiting,

But you are all that I want when it comes to being with you, no matter where we have come from, no matter where we go, it will always be you,

The music comes to a melodic end and then there's silence. Scared for a few moments to open my eyes, I hear the studio door open and close. I slowly open my eyes, feeling my body start to shake. His eyes are hooded and I look at him apprehensively, he is unreadable, and I clear my throat.

"It's a mash-up of different songs through the ages with my spin on it… it's about you." I feel so nervous as this is not only about my A-level piece, I have just sung my heart out. And whether he realises it or not, I love him so much it hurts through to the depth of my soul.

I have never felt so vulnerable in my life.

Before I know it, we are standing far too close and all I can hear is our ragged breathing. He pushes back a strand of my hair behind my ear, meeting my eyes, staying silent, he leans in slowly, his mouth hovering over mine, my lips part, anticipating the kiss. His lips gently brush mine as if he is testing his limits. I think it is the most erotic manoeuvre I have ever felt.

Then his lips crash onto mine with such an intense kiss, it steals my breath and I drop the headphones to the floor. My heartbeat spikes and I need to remember to breathe, otherwise I am going to pass out.

His hands tangle in my hair, trying to pull me closer, deeper, his tongue eases gently into my mouth and I can't help but moan. I wrap my arms around him and softly stroke the arch of his neck, my whole body craves this and relaxes so easily into his touch, into him, he makes me feel whole. I push my tongue into his perfect mouth, wanting to taste all of him and I will take anything he will give me. He lets out a small moan and I love hearing that sound from him. He pulls back slowly and puts a gentle peck on my nose, but all I want is more.

"I knew you could do it; you are so talented." He kisses the top of my head and pulls me closer, and holds me for a few moments. My whole-body buzzes with excitement, his eyes sparkling, ah you let down, hormones, brain help my heart as it has been sent into a frenzy. Does this mean he likes the song, or that he feels the same way?

"You like it?" I whisper out loud.

Am I ready for the truth?

He nods his head against me. It's times like this I wish I was more of a stubborn person, so I could keep away from him. My stomach clenches – how I would love to reciprocate this into something more and rip his clothes off.

Keep your cool, Cora, you've got this.

Only one more week of this and then, and then I would never have to see him again. Tears threaten to escape my eyes, and I blink them back. The thought makes me want to vomit with sadness. I turn my head, so it's burrowed into his neck, wanting to remember him, how he smelt, how this felt. I can feel his pulse beating wildly, and the smell of his mint and citrus cologne fills my senses. That smell immediately turns me on, hell, just looking at him from afar turns me on.

"Did you just smell me?" His grip on me tightens, he stiffens and lets out a defeated sigh.

"No," I laugh nervously.

"Cora, I know that we shouldn't, not here, but I don't know if I can stop myself any longer, I can't do this any longer."

"What happens if I don't care?" He pulls away so slightly, his face torn, searching my eyes, and he presses his forehead onto mine. I feel like I could explode with the amount of sexual tension that runs between us. Can he really be thinking we can be more than the desired look and wanting? Can we be together? Is sex on the cards again? I know it was my first time and I do not have nothing to compare it to, but *it* was downright hot. He plants another soft, slow kiss on my lips, and I pull him close.

Why are we never able to stop ourselves?

Surely this is a sign, fate, that our star signs are aligned? And of course, his phone starts to ring. That stupid phone! He pulls away quickly and answers it.

"Hello?" I can hear a woman on the other end of the phone, something about Amy.

Who's Amy?

"Okay, right, thank you for letting me know, I will be there right away." He hangs up and quickly looks at me. "We will have to continue this session later in the week Cora, I have to go." He starts gathering his things and shooing me out of the studio.

"Is everything okay?"

"Erm, yes, just a forgotten doctor's appointment. But I need to leave now."

"A doctor's appointment... with Amy?" I see his face drop and I look at him curiously. "Who's Amy?"

"It is none of your business," he replies coldly. Wow, if that had come out any meaner, it could have been deemed a slap. And his wall goes back up.

"Is she your girlfriend?" I blurt out. He stops what he is doing and looks at me, his eyes expressionless.

"No. Now I need to go; you can see yourself out."

With that, he leaves the room. This is why he doesn't want to continue; he has a girlfriend or worse, a wife.

Twenty-One

Silence on the Western Front — Cora

The next day, I wake up feeling angry. The way he was so rude to my face yesterday, how dare he talk to me like that. I know his life isn't any of my business, but I thought he was different and at least treated me with respect. Yet, he just cast me aside like I meant nothing. I even gave into temptation, another mind-blowing kiss, and then his emotions ran cold. I texted him, asking if he was okay. I wasn't proud of myself and felt really shitty when I woke up this morning because he hadn't even texted me back.

I wasn't surprised, but I felt hurt, again.

When I arrive at school, I decide that this time I will demand an explanation and tell him I can't keep going like this either. I was living by his moods and what he wanted. I just felt so stupid, such a child, I felt worthless. I wanted out for real this time; love shouldn't hurt this much. When entering the Music room to finish my exam I am ready for the biggest fallout of my life, I am ready for the end of this relationship. But on arrival, the other Music teacher, Mr Glen, is in the music room.

"Where's Mr Jones? He is supposed to work with me on my piece."

"He has called in sick today, a family emergency. But never fear, he has saved the pieces on the system and emailed the rest of the tasks to complete this morning, so we can pick up where he left off."

I inwardly explode as I let out a growl. Mr Glen looks at me confused, and then continues setting up the exam. What the heck! 'Family emergency,' how can he not even be here and he hasn't even texted me or said anything,

I feel totally dumped.

It takes me several minutes to calm down, as I even out my breathing and then settle down to the task at hand. I put the words to my last song – this composition was a little slower, with very simple notes used to help my voice carry the tune. The music starts and I pour my heart and soul into this, my emotions are all over the place.

The trees behind my house are alive, mmmmmmmmmmm, yeahhhhhhhhhh

In Spring they sing to one another, they chatter, they dance.

The bright, green leaves rustle and the cherry blossom explodes with happiness,

The trees behind my house are alive, mmmmmmmmmmm, yeahhhhhhhhhh

In summer they cry, the scorched sky, the burnt grass,

Where is all the rain?

The trees behind my house are alive, mmmmmmmmmmm, yeahhhhhhhhhh

In Autumn, they undress, they shake away the year,

Holding on to a promise that the next season will be better,

The trees behind my house are alive, mmmmmmmmmmm, yeahhhhhhhhhh

Standing tall, bare, they whisper along the frost,

Holding hands, breathing in the new year,

The trees behind my house are alive, mmmmmmmmmmmm, yeahhhhhhhhhh

I surprise myself as I sing with such a raspy, melancholy voice, trying to hold in my cry. Even though I finish my piece, I feel restless that the song is not up to my usual standard. And that just made me rage inside even more because this was the reason why I wanted to stay away from him. I did not want my grades to suffer, and this is precisely what is happening.

After an hour, the music is completed and sequenced to the server, ready to send off to the examination board and I cannot wait to leave. Mr Glen is all compliments, saying I had a natural gift with music, which is lovely, but it sounded so much more coming from Zach. I know what I have to do, I need to cross the line and figure out what's happening because I am starting to go crazy, and I feel like I am living up to dickhead Stefan's outburst of me! So, I do what any sane person would, and I drive to my teacher's house. I am relieved to see his car on his drive. I need to know where I stand with this, I need to know now!

I walk up to the door, legs shaking and pulse racing. I need to get my breathing under control before I have a panic attack. I hover over the doorbell and then change my mind and start to walk away, before talking myself into going back to the door.

If anyone looked out their window now, they'd think there was a mad woman moving away and then back to the door. "Call the police," Mavis would say as she peered through her net curtain. "That woman is talking to herself and walking to and from the door!"

I knock on the door lightly, crossing the line, crossing the line, crossing the line. Zach opens the door, in low-cut jeans and a thick woollen jumper, his hair looks freshly washed, and he has the 5-o'clock shadow covers his strong jaw and I clench my legs together and try not to salivate.

His face falls, and a wash of emotions floods his face: hurt, anger and disappointment.

Ouch.

"Cora," he squeaks. He pulls the porch door shut. He looks like he's just been caught out, making my stomach tie in knots. "What are you doing here?" I see he folds his arms immediately.

Eek, the body language is dire.

"You ran out of class yesterday as if your life depended on it. Family emergency, said Mr Glen, and I was, you know... worried." He opens his mouth to respond, then closes it again.

"Is that the *McDonald's*?" I hear a shout from the living room. I look at him, horrified; it is another woman. I see him close his eyes and breathe in.

Busted! I am done with this!

Without warning, I barge past him and into his house. I open the door to the living room, and there, lying on the sofa with a cast on, is a young girl. She looks at me with a warm smile and I can see the resemblance immediately.

Is this his daughter?

Oh, jeez, it's worse than I thought, another woman and they have a kid together. I look at him perplexed and he seems a little annoyed at my jealous rampage. He closes the front door and walks into the living room.

"Amy, this is Cora. Cora, this is Amy."

She smiles at me and waves. "Are you having dinner with us too?" I look back at Zach again, so confused.

"She is my daughter," he adds.

My eyes feel like they are going to explode out of my head. He has a daughter; how did he fail to mention this? We stand looking at each other. I can see he is wanting an explanation for me being in his house and I want the same back from him. I guess this is a stand-off. I have years of practice, you ain't gonna win, mister! The doorbell goes again and Zach leaves the room. I look back at Amy, what is she, six or seven years old? How old was Zach when he became a dad, fifteen years old? He became a dad, younger than I am now, is that even possible?

Of course, it is, as I shake that ridiculous thought out of my head. Where is the mum, are they still together, is he married? I have so many questions. I have *all* the questions.

"Do you like my cast, Cora?" I snap out of my running commentary and the million thoughts that are firing through my brain and walk over to the sofa and sit next to her.

"I love it, what happened?"

"Fell off the trim trail yesterday at school, I had to go to the hospital. I stayed there alllllllllll night! I had an X-ray, and they said it was broken. They put the wet stuff on it and now it's hard, feel it, feel it, Cora." I do as she says and then smile at her.

"It feels like wood." Her green eyes light up in delight. I love her already.

"I have lots of glitter pens, would you like to draw on it?"

"I would love that." I start to draw a unicorn on it and Amy grabs another pen and draws with me. Zach re-enters the room and I look up and smile, but he still looks super unhappy, he walks over to Amy with a soft smile.

"Here is your Happy Meal, kiddo."

"Thanks, Dadad. Look at what Cora is drawing, it's a unicorn, isn't it pretty?"

He sits on the coffee table close to me. If looks could kill, I think there would be a crime scene about now, blood and guts all over the floor, murder by death eyes!

"It is beautiful." He sits and watches me draw until I have finished.

"You're a good drawer. Do you work together?" Amy asks, breaking the silence.

"Sort of." He jumps in.

"Look at my X-rays." She shows me some small pictures. "Dadad took them on his phone when the doctor didn't look, he is so funny."

"Well, that is cheeky," I smile back.

"We are watching *Aladdin,* have you seen it? I love Jasmin, she's my favourite. Who is your favourite princess?" I try to concentrate on finishing the drawing. I see that Zach's leg is bouncing. He is stressed – good!

"Probably *Moana,* strong, confident, what more can I ask for in a *Disney* character?" She nods in agreement and traces the unicorn after I finish.

"Daddy loves *The Lion King*. I think this is my favourite drawing, much better than Daddy's stick man here," she shows a very badly-drawn picture and I let out a little laugh.

"Well, thank you both for abusing my artistic drawings, you wee madame, eat your dinner and I am going to show Cora out, as she has to go home now."

Busted again!

"Ohhhhhhhhhhhh, okay, Daddy. Bye, Cora, can you come back soon?"

"Sure." I smile as if Zach will let me anywhere near him again, which at this moment, with how he is ushering me out the front room and to the door, looks doubtful. He switches up the volume on the TV and closes the front room door softly behind him.

He glares at me.

"Cora, this is unacceptable and an absolute invasion of my privacy," he angrily whispers.

"And you turning up at my door wasn't?" He doesn't say anything but stares coldly at me. "I'm sorry, okay, I was worried... why wouldn't you say you had a daughter?"

"Why? Why? Because it's none of your bloody business, that's why." He opens the door quickly; I have never seen him so furious. This is bad, really bad. I step out of the door.

"I just don't understand why you would want to hide this from me. Is it because you are still with the mum?" If he looked furious before, I have no idea what the word is now. I think borderline killer rage.

"Goodbye Cora."

He shuts the door in my face. I stand there for a few seconds, trying to process what happened. He shut the door in my face, he just shut the door in my face.

HE SHUT THE DOOR IN MY FACE.

Rude!

I let out the loudest groan of frustration. I storm back to my car and road rage all the way home, putting on the screamiest music I own. *System of Down* and *P.O.D.* just about did it. Flipping off any driver that came near me and swearing loudly at everything so that when I arrive home, the anger has gone from boiling point to gentle simmering. I didn't want Dad to see me like this and worry. How can he be such a gorgeous human being and turn into an absolutely confusing crap bag?

Ahhhh! I don't even know what he is. He has a daughter. He must have been, what, fifteen or sixteen years old when he had Amy?

Why is it that even when he is so angry with me, he is so pretty damn sexy? I literally run to my room and faceplant onto the bed, screaming into it, crying big, fat tears. He makes me feel so inadequate, he lied to me, he has all this power over me, and that has to change, no one controls me.

Why is he so confusing and a gorgeous man?

I am now completely done. Being a grown-up hurts and falling in love is too hard!

Twenty-Two

After she left – Zach

I was awake most of the night thinking of her, nothing unusual there then. I was so mad at her for turning up and I couldn't contain my exploding rage. I also thought sleeping with her would have calmed my thoughts, but it hadn't. In fact, I think it made it worse.

I have never wanted anyone as I want her.

I really don't understand why I feel like this, my life is in some sort of order, like a mask I have hidden behind so well, for so long and she, well she sees right through it. I feel off, not right, scared even. It makes me feel as if I am not safe, loving someone else, opening my heart again... I can't, they might die. It shocks me how much I want her and how much I feel for her. I realised straight away how I behaved was totally irrational and definitely brought out the overprotective father in me. It wasn't my finest hour, shutting the door in her face. I don't want anyone getting too close to Amy, hurting her, not again. She has had enough hurt in her short life already. As a dad, that's my job, to protect her, but being an arse about it is not and I am not an arse.

The next day, I couldn't take it anymore, I had to text her, but say what? Father in the house, or, sorry I lied that I am a dad? Oops, I slammed the door in your face... nothing seemed right. I started feeling aggravated and snappy, and poor Amy got the brunt of it, she even noticed.

"Dadad, are you okay? You seem sad today, is it because of my leg?"

I smile at her as we watch another *Disney* movie. "No, it is not, just some things at work that are hard to do and it makes me cross."

"Well, when I am cross you tell me to shout into a pillow or take deep breaths, do you think that will help you, Daddy?"

"Maybe." I sigh, looking at my phone again for the tenth time this hour. It's not as if looking at the damn thing will make her text me back, and I do not even know what to say if we ever spoke again. My hurt pangs with sadness, *if* I ever see her again.

"Is that girl going to come around again? She's nice, I like her and her drawing. Why do you not bring any of your friends home, Daddy? I bring all my friends home for tea, maybe she can come for tea?"

"Maybe... I tell you what, I will text and ask her." I grab my phone and text her.

Hey, sorry about yesterday, Amy really likes the picture you drew for her.

Sending that message, it felt a bit of a relief, that I was reaching out, that I was trying. I busied myself for the rest of the day. I took Amy to a follow-up appointment at the hospital, purposely driving the long way through town and driving slower than normal. I told myself I was driving steady for Amy's leg but it was really to see if I could see Cora walking somewhere. I needed to get a grip, trying to look for her, when I didn't even know where she was.

After I carried Amy to bed and read her three stories, she was finally asleep. I went to the fridge, pulled out a beer, made myself comfortable on the sofa and watched some footie I had recorded from the weekend. It had been a whole day, and I could see she had read my message, but still no reply. After an hour in and a few beers later, I had the courage to text her again.

I get that you do not want to talk to me, but I am really sorry. Please at least give me the chance to explain...

Still, nothing and I could see she had read it straight away. She didn't turn up to her last tutor session with me later that week, but I found out from the other teacher that she'd finished up her last tutor group with him the day before.

I felt like shit now.

So, this was it, I was officially not her teacher anymore. I debated whether to listen to her other song. In the end, I couldn't resist, I had to hear it. As I listened to her song in the recording studio. I couldn't breathe. It was called, *The Tree of Life*. Her husky voice was like a siren, it pulled me in, and it was pure raw emotion. She was so musically gifted, it made me feel I was right with her on the journey. Before I knew it, I was crying, over a fucking tree. But I knew it was more than that, it feels as if I have lost her, and I wipe my tears away quickly.

I sit for a while, unsure of what to think anymore. I haven't slept properly in days, not so much about Cora, but Amy was uncomfortable and needed pain relief at all hours of the night. Thankfully my aunt had come over and was staying for a few days to let me actually sleep. Suddenly, out of nowhere, I feel utter relief; the weight of the world has been lifted off my shoulders and it really sank in. I wasn't her teacher anymore, she was just a woman, and I was just a man, like before, in the pub. I could actually let myself like her, which wasn't a problem; I did really like her. I didn't have to feel bad or guilty, well...not as much. I text her again;

The song is perfect

But the text came back undeliverable, without a thought, I rang her, but her phone had been disconnected... oh.

Twenty-Three

The space in between – Cora

Several days later, Dad and I sit at the kitchen table. It is Saturday lunchtime and we are happily munching on a salmon and feta cheese salad, which I have prepared. Dad is recovering well; he is up and about around the house and looking more like himself. We had a follow-up visit from the hospital yesterday, the doctors were pleased with his progress. They said with some physiotherapy, he could return to work in September (but part-time). He must continue to take it easy, to aim for a better diet, more exercise and a work-life balance. Otherwise, the doctor said that he could be back in the same situation again in five years, if not sooner. If that isn't a wake-up call, I do not know what is.

"Dad, how do you stop liking someone?"

He looks at me, surprised. I had received Zach's messages and decided I couldn't do it anymore. I deserved more, I deserved better, and he could not offer me that. This relationship we had was so messy before it even got started. The continual struggle with keeping up with what he wanted and what I wanted. He was so hot and so cold and also a dad, not that it mattered, in fact, I don't know how, but it made him hotter.

Maybe I have daddy issues.

So, I did what any sensible 18-year-old would, I got blindly drunk at a friend's house (insert Sophie here), cried a lot and then blocked his number. The next morning, I told Dad that the issues hadn't stopped at school and needed a new number and voila, a new phone, a new number and no Zach. Problem is, I had semi-memorised his number, which I was trying very hard to forget. My heart hurt so much, and it felt like he had died. I read the poetry book he gave me a few weeks back from start to finish. Then, I read it at least another ten times. Those poems spoke to me on all kinds of levels and he was not wrong, they helped in guiding me emotionally. They made me realise that it was okay to feel this way and that I wasn't alone in this journey.

"Who do I need to kill?"

"Ha, very funny Dad," I respond, "I am serious, how? How did you get over Mum?"

"I fell in love with a guy."

"Again, not helpful." He sits there for a moment and ponders the question more seriously.

He sighs, "Although I am not thrilled you've decided to start dating, I think to get over someone, I would say time, a change in habit. But if you really want to analyse it, think about why you are not good for each other. Things don't work out for a reason my love, and I think it can be anything. Not wanting the same things, you could be at different points in your life that don't quite connect, and you disagree on the silliest thing like money. Honestly, it could be anything, only you can work this one out. Love is not rational; love is messy and ridiculous. But to love fearlessly without wanting to change, without wanting them to be different, is exhilarating and frightening. But darling, what is the point in being with someone if we can't be free to feel these things, to be yourself? You are too young for all this yet, but one day, I hope you will find this for yourself, just like I did with your Mum. And even though it didn't work out, I do not regret any of it, as I have you and Daisy, and that is more than I can ever ask for."

My dad is such a romantic. We sit in silence for a few moments, and I think about why Zach and I are no good for each other, and if I think with my adult head, I know that it would never work. We are at totally different stages of our lives, and the thing is he didn't even want to try; he wasn't honest with me, and he was my teacher. My poor lustful heart and my poor vagina will never be the same again.

"So, Prom next week, did you order that dress online?" Dad asks, interrupting my thoughts. I nod.

"Yes, and it fits perfectly."

I had spent hours internet shopping for the perfect prom dress. Funny how many hours you can spend looking at utter nonsense in a hospital when there is not much to do but sit and wait. I had many hours to research the perfect dress and it was just that. A beautiful deep green silk ballgown with a plunge V-neck and twist straps with a low back. It hugged all the right places, and I had smoky green eye shadow to go with it.

I was aiming for perfection.

Dad had also said I could get my hair and nails done, so of course I said yes! I decided that my hair would be styled into a side twist and curled, and boy did I look like a proper grown-up. When the artist had finished the trial for my face and hair, I didn't even recognise myself, and that is exactly what I want to be.

Someone different, someone new.

Twenty-Four

Her Prom — Cora

L ooking good, feeling good. School Prom is here. All exams finished last week and this is a momentous occasion for me. But my thoughts wander to Mum and I wish she was here. It was hard seeing all my other classmates with their mum's. Don't get me wrong, Dad did a great job with the photos and the limo. He really did splash out and showed lots of attention and love, gushing at the right moments and saying how amazing I looked.

But I still miss her.

As we pull up to the hotel entrance, all thoughts of her disappear and I am oddly excited and relieved that this is the last time I have to see all these people and I never have to go to school again.

That is music to my ears.

It has been a bittersweet experience. However, I am glad that Sophie and I have chosen each other as dates. We link arms and walk into the hotel function room like we own the joint.

"Cee Cee, you look so bloody gorgeous tonight, you are making me rethink the whole man thing, I think I want to swap sides." I laugh, and we hug. "We made it. School can officially go do one!"

She gives me a kiss on the cheek and takes one more quick selfie and heads to the mocktail bar. It makes me laugh because I think Sophie has drunk a whole bottle of vodka, and by the looks of most of the pupils here, they have done the same.

I decided to not drink tonight, after the hangover I had the other week, which I swear I can still feel in my bones. I was a complete mess and crying, I didn't want that to be my last memory of my school experience, drunk and vomiting, saying or doing something I may regret.

I am sober and proud.

I survey the room, letting my eyes roam and like energy drawn together, I lock eyes with Zach and we stare just a beat too long. Ah crap, he is obviously on the Prom committee as an adult chaperone. Jeez, he looks beautiful in his grey sculpted suit. He doesn't look like he has shaved for a few days either, drool. Time stands still as we devour each other's bodies with our eyes. I stop myself from looking away, letting my heart pine for him, letting myself feel the loss, feel the grief. It feels like the crowd just fades away for a moment and it's just me and him. He would walk over and ask to dance, and he would just hold me as we slowly moved around the room together. He would accidentally step on my toe, and we would laugh because this is what couples do, silly romantic things together. He would kiss me on my forehead, tell me he loves me, and all would be right with the world.

Oh, brain, I do love your fantasies, they have definitely helped me through these past five months, don't ever change. This will be the last time I 'officially' have to see him. So, I am glad that I went all out tonight because I want to show him what he is missing out on, and by the look on his face, it seems it has done the job. He is making sex eyes at me for once, and his mouth looks like it might hit the floor. Then, Stefan grabs me.

"Hi, gorgeous." He smiles. "Let's dance." He pulls me to the dance floor, not waiting for an answer. Clearly, he has had a lot to drink as he is dancing all over the place, which makes me laugh for a moment.

He is an awful dancer. But then I remember what a dickhead he is. The music slows, of bloody course it does, and he pulls me close. He smells like beer as his heavy breath lands on my face. "You look amazing and I am sorry I said we slept together," he mumbles in a slurred voice. Yep, he is still a dick and I still feel nothing, no spark, no internal wash of pleasure or joy with the compliments. Just hate and disgust. I see Zach watching me out of the corner of my eye as I feel Stefan's hands slip so low, he is grabbing my bum.

FFS.

I pull away. He is grinning wildly and pulls me roughly in for a very wet kiss. I push him away. Clearly, this boy has a problem.

"What the hell, Stefan, I told you before."

"You give me mixed signals!" He shouts.

"I have given you no signals, we are not even friends, and you are a bell end."

"You are a cock tease."

I let out a frustrated sigh, ready to punch him in his whole face again, but I know that it doesn't matter, after today. I do not have to see anyone again if I don't want to. I start to walk away; he just is not worth it and I want to go home. Being here was a mistake, my heart hurts too much for this, and I do not want to be sad anymore. I search the room for his beautiful face, so I can mentally say goodbye, but I cannot see him.

I close my eyes and whisper my goodbye.

I let Sophie know I am leaving, making some bull up about my dad needing me at home. She makes no attempt to stop me as she is already eyeing up someone on the dance floor, so I quickly nip to the toilet before I leave.

A few minutes later, as I slip out the side door from the main hall, something catches my eye and I stop. Stefan and Sophie are kissing on the dance floor. I choke back a laugh, and then sadness fills my stomach. Is he a crap person, or is she? It shouldn't bother me, but surely there is a kissing law? Or a friend code to not kiss the dickhead who has mentally given me crap for the last few months?

I shrug, *fuck it*, I am done anyway.

I leave feeling happy to draw a line under all of this and disappear out the side door. The rain is pouring, and it drenches me immediately. I gasp in shock and curse myself for not bringing a coat or umbrella. But then I look up at the sky and open my arms out and shout,

"Bring it on, fuckers!" I laugh wildly, take my shoes off, and throw them towards the car I parked in the car park earlier. I close my eyes, enjoying this moment. Smelling the spring rain has always been a firm favourite. I feel free and happy, no more school, no more!

I received my provisional online acceptance for my university today. Starting in September, I will be going to the music school in London, and now, now I get to officially begin again.

Twenty-Five

His Prom — Zach

I roam her body greedily; she looks unbelievably stunning. She runs right out into the warm rain. Thank goodness it's May. She looks shocked and then she throws her head back and enjoys it (even though I just saw Stefan kiss her again. It annoyed me, after everything he said about her). I can't help but laugh at her stupidity.

Who enjoys the rain?

I don't mean to stare, but she doesn't see me at first and she looks so happy and carefree. I miss her already. She suddenly opens her eyes and turns to me; she must have felt my eyes upon her.

"I guess you saw that?" I smile at her. "Guess you saw Stefan kiss me again too?"

"Yep, just needed some air."

Clenching my fists, I try to push the anger and the jealousy down, but it was becoming a real problem of late. And she wasn't even mine. She can see my conflicting emotions and sort of nods and walks to pick up her shoes.

She is absolutely soaking and her dress is clung to every inch of her curves. It makes her look sensational and my dick twinges – down boy, this is not the right time. I walk to her and offer her a space under my umbrella. Selfish really, wanting to be close to her, wanting to see if I can see through the dress, remembering her naked body.

"I am not your teacher anymore," I start. She looks at me with a face so unreadable.

"Cora, talk to me."

"I don't think this is the right time or place." I didn't care; this couldn't wait.

"I texted you a few times."

"Yeah, I got them." She starts to walk away.

"I just want to explain... will you let me explain... please?"

Her eyes soften and I take that as a yes. We walk back to the undercover part and she sits beside me on the wooden bench in the hotel courtyard. I keep the umbrella up to give us some privacy and I give her a small hopeful smile.

Where do I even start?

I look at how beautiful she is and remember how thoughtful she was when I was feeling low about my mum. I decide that it is time to tell the truth, to just let her see me, to finally let my guard down. I offer my jacket, which she takes gratefully, and I stare at her for a few moments, pushing her damp hair from her face, she pulls back slightly by my public display of effection. "So, my secret is out, I am a dad. I didn't mean to hide it from you or from anyone, really. You just have to understand, being a young dad, and a teenage dad, people treated me differently. I think some people didn't mean to, but I could see it when they looked at me. Sometimes, people even made remarks about my situation. I had to deal with all of this whilst I was still at school, then juggling university. I had this baby; it was hard for us. I have had to deal with that for me and for Amy. I had to protect us, it is my responsibility to love her and protect her, and I want to do that for her; she is my daughter."

I take a moment before I continue.

"Sarah, her mum, we were a thing at school, and I guess we thought we loved each other. Anyway, I will spare the sordid details, but she became pregnant. She was horrified, she was raised in a strong Catholic household, so when her family found out, they did not want anything to do with her. That broke Sarah, and I had to convince her to keep the baby because I knew that the baby was meant to be. I couldn't end an innocent child's life, and I knew deep down inside she wouldn't be able to live with herself either.

She moved in with my mum and me, but when Amy was born, Sarah told me right away she did not want her, she did not want to be her mum. She only carried her for my sake, again another awful story, but in short, she left, returned home and gave me full custody. My mum was amazing with Amy, we both loved her so much, and she was and is perfect. And even though I tried to contact Sarah over the first few years of Amy's life, I would send her letters, and pictures, but they all came back unopened and I decided that we both didn't need the heartache, so I stopped."

I hesitate a moment and sigh.

"When Mum started to get sick, it was so hard for all of us. Amy was only 4, but she is so smart, she knew what was happening. When my mum died, it wasn't just me that was heartbroken. Amy was distraught. To see my child so sad was an unbelievable pain. That's when I moved here, to be closer to my aunt, my mum's sister. I thought it might help Amy, and it did, in a way, for both of us. I was so utterly lost and we both needed a support network. It took months before she stopped crying in the day, but the night crying, the night crying that has only just stopped over the last few months. We both felt the loss so badly. She only has me and my aunt left."

I pause, sighing again.

"Look, I am sorry I shut you out. I guess that the only way I have been able to deal with more heartbreak is to not let anyone in, or, get close to people. I felt so confused and conflicted. But I am done pretending this is nothing. I have tried so hard to get you out of my head, I have tried to forget you and… I can't. I really care about you and I know you care about me."

I look at Cora. She is staring at her floor with tears in her eyes. I place my hand over hers, the silence slowly eating me up.

"Please, say something," I whisper.

"What do you want me to say? I would never ask you to throw away this, any of this. But you thought that I would judge you?" She replies sternly.

"I saw the look on your face when I told you I was Amy's dad, the look of judgement from all people, I did not expect that from you." She scoffs.

"You've done nothing but judge me since that day I walked into your classroom – that's really hypocritical."

"What position am I in? I have everything to lose."

"And I don't? My dad's the acting head teacher here."

"I don't have my shit together," I confess.

"…And I do?"

"That is not what I am saying, will you please stop arguing with me and listen? You are so damn infuriating!" I did not intend to use my teacher's voice, and I see that she is taken aback by my sharp response. "I know I can't make you forgive me, no matter how sorry I am, I just wanted you to know. I thought that you deserved the truth if this is the last time we are going to see each other. I just can't have you going out into the world, knowing that you hate me."

She lets out a wee laugh and sighs as she sits up straight and stares into my eyes. A tear escapes her eye and she wipes it away like it's nothing.

"Hate you? I don't hate you; I bloody love you, yet you are so wrapped up in yourself, you do not even see it. You do not even see me." Her words feel like the wind has been knocked from my soul. Does she love me? When did this happen?

"That…That's not true." I look away, tormented.

"Yes, it is," she touches my cheek softly and guides my face to look at her. "Because if you truly saw me, you would have given me a chance, you would have told me… you know what, I don't even care you have a kid. Amy seems so nice. But you pigeonholed me like everyone else. You thought that I would judge you or look at you differently, which may I add, was a surprised face when I saw Amy. Not a face of judgement. It's a fact that you didn't even give me that chance. You didn't tell me, or show me who you truly are. You didn't even want to give me that chance, you didn't even want to try. That's what hurts. So, no, I don't hate you, Zach… I've just realised that I am not enough for you, and I guess, I guess that has to be okay."

We stare at each other. What have I done, what have I lost? Was she right? Was she enough for me, or my daughter, for both of us? But I had no answer because she was right. I hadn't let her try; I hadn't given us a chance. I had closed myself off to the fear of being left alone again, so it ended up coming true and I was being left again. But even worse, I was alone again because I hadn't even tried. The sorrow flits across her face as I search her eyes for more, but I can't shake that nagging feeling that this is it. I know I am not any good at sharing my feelings or emotions or even being in relationships. I have closed myself off. I do not know how to do it anymore and this is the end.

The music from the hall dances along the breeze and we both realise where we are. She stands and I mirror her actions. I pull her into a hug because if this is the last time I get to see her, the last time I get to touch her, I want to make it last for as long as possible. I wanted her close. I breathe in her scent, not wanting to let her go, her damp dress presses against me, and I feel her slightly shaking.

"Goodbye, Zach," she whispers in my ear.

As I reluctantly let go, she kisses me softly on the cheek, hands me back my jacket and walks away.

She never looks back.

Shit.

Twenty-Six

Epilogue

W hat will happen now Cora has left?

What will Zach do? Find out in the sequel...

"... And the Second" is available now on Amazon.

https://mybook.to/urpaB

Here is a little sneak peek ...

Zach ...

That was not telling her my feelings, that was showing her I couldn't control myself. We needed to sit down like rational adults and talk about it. I needed to get my head out of my kecks and think like a man on a mission and my mission was her. I was going to make her mine. Whatever it takes.

Cora ...

My thoughts kept me awake most of the night, thinking of how this evening could have ended up so much worse. Adam is such a great guy and I am annoyed Zach had ruined me for any other man. And as dawn broke, there was one thing that I had decided. If I ever see that god-like man again, Zach Jones. I will kick him in his beautiful face and then chop off his perfect dick!

Let's be friends!

Don't forget to follow me on Instagram: https://www.instagram.com/hb_publishing_house

Don't forget to follow me on Facebook: https://www.facebook.com/hb publishinghouse

Don't forget to follow me on TikTok: https://www.tiktok.com/@hbpubli shinghouse

Like and subscribe to my story page on YouTube: https://www.youtube.com/@timeforastory

Visit: www.hbpublishinghouse.co.uk

Acknowledgments

To all the people who have made this book a reality, thank you, you know who you are. To my husband, for letting me escape up to the attic so I can write like a mad woman. Thank you to my work wife for all the chats, inspiration, cups of tea, reading random words and listening to me whittle. To my children for letting me have five more minutes to type the next paragraph. Thank you to Read by Rose for editing this book, Harry for creating a beautiful book cover and HB publishing house for giving me a chance. And to you, the readers, I hope you enjoy this journey.

Rob Dial Junior, The Mindset Mentor

The Grief We're Given Poems by William Bortz

Printed in Great Britain
by Amazon

23667313R00108